P9-DMJ-626

THE BATTLE OF DARCY LANE

THE BATTLE OF DARCY LANE

TARA ALTEBRANDO

RP|KIDS
PHILADELPHIA • LONDON

Books published by Running Press are available at special discounts
for bulk purchases in the United States by corporations, institutions,
and other organizations. For more information, please contact the
Special Markets Department at the Perseus Books Group,
2300 Chestnut Street, Suite 200, Philadelphia, PA 19103, or
call (800) 810-4145, ext. 5000, or e-mail
special.markets@perseusbooks.com.

ISBN 978-0-7624-4948-4

Library of Congress Control Number: 2013946377

E-book ISBN 978-0-7624-5199-9

9 8 7 6 5 4 3 2 1
Digit on the right indicates the number of this printing

Designed by T.L. Bonaddio
Cover art by T.L. Bonaddio
Edited by Lisa Cheng
Typography: Pupcat, Museo Sans, and Museo Slab

Published by Running Press Kids
An Imprint of Running Press Book Publishers
A Member of the Perseus Books Group
2300 Chestnut Street
Philadelphia, PA 19103–4371

Visit us on the web!
www.runningpress.com/kids

FOR ELLIE AND VIOLET

1.

Taylor and I were sitting on my front porch
pretending to be millionaires as the afternoon turned into
evening. It was only the second week of summer vacation
and already boredom was like a pesky mosquito that we
were swatting away.

"Only boring people get bored," my mom had already
said like a hundred times. "Life's what you make it."

We'd spent the day in my pool and lounging on the
deck out back, and planting some seeds in my vegetable
garden, then playing tetherball and now Millionaire. From
where we sat on the swinging bench, with tall glasses of
lemonade, there was still no sign of the cicadas and it was
like the whole of Darcy Lane—the whole town, too—was
holding its breath.

Dad was predicting there would be mayhem—car crashes caused by swarms, that sort of thing—when the huge, beady-eyed bugs finally showed. My mom, a teacher, was mostly interested in the educational aspect of the whole spectacle. I was lucky I hadn't officially been quizzed yet—about the cicada's life cycle, about the forty-three countries where people eat them like popcorn.

I was in believe-it-when-I-see-it mode. Which, come to think of it, was how most people on the block had felt about the rumor that people were finally going to be moving into the new house across the street. But here, at long last, were our new neighbors. So at least *something* was happening.

"She looks like she might actually *work* for a living," I said, when the new mom appeared at their front door.

Taylor fanned herself with a magazine. "Oh, the poor woman!"

"There goes the neighborhood!" I said, and we laughed in a fake-stuffy, rich person way. This was pretty much how you played Millionaire.

Right then, the movers—who had so far carried in a lot of boxes plus a very large television, an extremely large fish tank (empty), and a huge stuffed giraffe—pulled from the truck a plushy hot-pink chair with the name ALYSSA stitched into it so big we could read it from all the way across the street.

"Wow," I said.

"Yeah," Taylor said.

We were hoping that before dinner we'd get another glimpse of the new girl, whom we hadn't seen since about 4:00 p.m.—almost two hours ago—when she'd gotten out of a car and gone inside.

"My mom met the mom," Taylor said. "The grandmother died last week. They came home from the funeral yesterday, and the moving truck was waiting for them."

"Jeez," I said. One of my grandmothers, my mom's mom, had died a long time ago and I didn't really remember her.

Taylor stretched her legs out in front of her and I did the same. She flicked away a little pebble stuck to her calf and said, "Then because of all that rain yesterday afternoon, the movers couldn't move their stuff in because it would all get ruined, so they had to sleep on the floor last night."

Taylor looked horrified but I said, "Sounds sort of fun."

I thought about borrowing some of the details for our game, imagining a massive mansion and us with sleeping bags.

"Their grandmother *died*." Taylor rolled her eyes at me. "She was supposed to live with them and everything."

I rolled my eyes back, but not so that she could see.

I hadn't noticed anybody walking across the street—I'd been stirring my drink with my straw and thinking of funny things a rich person might say about lemonade—but then she was there, on the path leading up to my porch.

The new girl.

Taylor stood up.

2.

A little over a year ago, I had been the new girl moving onto the block and Taylor had come over to say hi. She'd shown me how to suck the nectar from the blossoms on the honeysuckle vines that grew through the fence next to her house and that had been that: best friends.

We hadn't been in any of the same classes at school last year, but after school and on weekends we'd been pretty inseparable—riding our bikes, playing cards, painting by numbers, and trying to flirt with Peter (me) and Andrew (Taylor) from the next street over. We were beyond excited to finally have the whole summer to just hang out again— and now we'd have a new person to do it with. Since our first sighting of the new girl, we'd been playing Millionaire,

yes, but also talking about the possibility of new clothes
to trade and borrow, and slumber parties in a house neither
of us actually lived in. Maybe the new girl even had cute
boy cousins from towns not so far away who'd come by all
the time for pool parties.

The new girl had long dark brown hair with the
sides pulled up to the top of her head in a butterfly clip, and
her top lip looked like it had been pinched and gotten
stuck in a permanent pucker.

"What are you doing?" she asked.

Taylor said, "We're just hanging out," before I had a
chance to explain that we were pretending to be millionaires.
"I'm Taylor and this is Julia."

The new girl studied us. "Are you sisters?"

Taylor pointed. "No. I live two houses down."

"Yeah, didn't think so."

It was true that Taylor and I looked nothing alike but for
some reason it sounded like an insult.

The new girl bounced a tennis ball I hadn't noticed in
her hand. "You don't really believe in unicorns, do you?"

The T-shirt I was wearing said SAVE THE UNICORN above
a drawing of one. "No," I said. "It's a joke."

"I don't get it." Then the new girl seemed to lose interest

12

because she said, "Do you guys know how to play Russia?"

"No." Taylor stood up and walked over to the top porch step, almost stepping on my foot. "How do you play?"

"First you go like this." The new girl threw the ball against my garage door and caught it. The sound was a deep *thump*.

"Anybody can do that," I said. I knew unicorns weren't real. I still liked the *idea* of them, though.

"Well, there are thirteen moves you have to do," the new girl said. "They get harder and harder, and you have to do the second move twice and the third move three times and so on. And if you drop the ball even once you have to start over with the first move. The first person to finish all the moves the right number of times without dropping the ball wins."

"Let me try," Taylor said, and the new girl threw her the ball.

"I'd rather sit here and count my piles of money," I said in my best fancy accent, but if either of them heard me, they didn't let on.

Taylor threw the ball against the wall and caught it.

Big deal, I thought. *Even a monkey could do that.* "Come on, Taylor. We were playing Millionaire!"

"What's *Millionaire*?" the new girl asked, and now she was the one that sounded snotty.

Taylor said, "Just a dopey game Julia made up."

"It's not dopey," I said, but nobody cared.

Taylor asked, "Hey, what's your name?" and the new girl answered, "Alyssa."

Then Alyssa started to talk and talk and talk, and we found out that she was twelve like us and that she'd moved from a town right across the bay. The house there had been really small and not that nice but her father had gotten a big promotion and then her grandmother had up and died and now here they were. Except her dad had left that morning for a business trip and pretty much traveled all the time.

"Wow," Taylor said.

"Yeah," I said. "Wow."

I looked away and did that eye-rolling thing again. I had a feeling there was going to be a lot of eye rolling now that Taylor was all gaga for Alyssa.

"So this time you let the ball bounce and then catch it." Alyssa took the ball back from Taylor and demonstrated. "It has to bounce between the wall and a line—like this line in the cement here—and if it goes out or you miss it, you have to start over with onesies. This is twosies. You do it twice."

"Twosies?" I snorted. "What are we, babies?" I put on a silly baby-talk voice. "Twosie, woosies. Coochie coochie coo."

I was about to say something about the stuffed giraffe we'd seen going into Alyssa's house because, really, who had stuffed animals at our age? But then I remembered the stuffed monkey Peter had given me for my birthday last year because he thought I was a good climber. There was also the not so small matter of my unicorn poster; Alyssa would like that about as much as she liked my shirt.

Taylor looked at me funny and turned to Alyssa—"Let me try"—and held her hand out for the ball, which Alyssa bounced to her. Taylor did the move twice. "Okay, what's next?" She bounced the ball back to Alyssa.

"Throw the ball in the air, clap three times, then catch." Alyssa did just that.

I had to hold back a snort.

Then someone we couldn't see but who must have been Alyssa's mother called her name.

"I gotta go." Alyssa snatched up her ball. "I guess I'll see you around, neighbors."

I watched her walk away, afraid to say anything before I knew she was out of earshot. And I worked hard to think of the exact right thing as I studied her hot pink tank top and too-tight, too-short shorts. Why did it feel like Alyssa had already lived on Darcy Lane forever and *I* was the new girl again?

"I don't know," I said after Alyssa disappeared into her house. "She seems sort of stuck up."

"I think she's cool," Taylor said with a longing look across the street.

"Cool?" I laughed.

"You're just jealous," Taylor said.

"Of *what*?"

Without my noticing her doing it, Taylor had moved her own clip from the back of her neck, where it had been holding her blonde hair in a low ponytail, to the same high position where Alyssa was wearing hers. She couldn't seem to find an answer to my question and only said, "Calm down, Julia."

"Why's the game called Russia anyway?" I blew hair out of my eyes with a quick puff.

"Don't know, don't care," Taylor said.

3.

"Big night for pizza," my mom said, after she pulled into the driveway and got out of the car. It was true she'd left a long time ago.

"Julia's dad's on his way," she said to Taylor, who was staying for dinner. We followed my mom inside as the empty moving truck pulled away.

My dad worked in the city at a company that built information systems for hospitals. He had to take a train then a ferry then another train from the office every day, and it seemed to me that the commute alone would be enough to make a person tired, never mind the working part. He came in right as we were sitting down with drinks, and before he even took his suit jacket off, he went to the fridge, got a beer, snapped the can open, and took a sip.

He handed it off to Mom, who also took a sip and put it on the table. They liked to share one at dinnertime.

"Well, hello, girls," he said, as if noticing us for the first time. He sat down at the table. "How was your day?"

"It was okay," I said.

"Just *okay*?" He loosened his tie and pulled it off with one long stretch of his arm. "I think a day spent lounging around playing cards and maybe going for a dip and drinking lemonade would be more than okay."

"I guess." I felt bad about him having to work all day.

"Oh! The people across the street moved in," Mom said. "I'll have to go over and introduce myself, maybe bring brownies." She reached for a slice of pizza.

Annoyed that my mom had reminded Taylor about the existence of Alyssa, I looked at Taylor, trying to read her expression. She was holding a slice, but I hadn't seen her take a bite yet. Taylor never ate much, and it showed in the way her ribs practically poked through her terry-cloth tube top.

"What are they like?" Dad asked, and it was Taylor who answered.

"There's a girl our age. She seems nice."

"Well, that's exciting, huh?" Dad looked at me.

"Yeah." My mouth was full of pizza. "It sure is."

"You shouldn't talk with your mouth full," Taylor said.

"Ah, well." Dad also had pizza in his mouth. "We all make mistakes, eh, Taylor?"

Man, I loved my dad.

"Their grandmother was going to live with them but she died last week," Taylor said.

"Oh, how awful." My mom's hand went to her heart.

"So!" Dad said with some fanfare. "You girls must be pretty excited for your big trip into the city on Saturday."

"Totally!" I said, even though there was still more pizza in my mouth. With all the excitement of the day I'd almost forgotten that Mom was taking us sightseeing and shopping. Taylor and I had been looking forward to it for weeks.

"Yeah." Taylor pulled some thick cheese off her slice. "Should be fun."

She didn't really sound like she meant it, but I didn't care. She'd see. It'd be awesome in every way.

"I just hope the cicadas hold off," Mom said. But the bugs were so late, supposedly because of the cold, wet spring we'd had, that I'd stopped believing they were ever going to come.

I called Taylor later and we talked about Saturday, like how we'd both ride in the backseat and pretend my mom was our chauffeur. She told me how her sister had called from the sleep-away camp where she was working as a counselor all summer to tell Taylor about her new boyfriend who had a motorcycle. We were so jealous. Then Taylor said, "I really miss her," and I said, "We'll have a great summer, don't worry." Everything felt right again.

A few minutes later, Taylor wanted to hang up to watch some new summer miniseries called *End of Daze* that was about to start. We decided that I'd go ring her bell when I was up the next day and we'd go for a morning swim.

"There's some big new miniseries starting tonight," I said when I walked into the den.

My parents were already in front of the TV. Each of them had a glass of red wine on the table beside them, which meant that this was some kind of big occasion.

"Julia," Mom said before I even had a chance to sit down on the couch next to her. "You have to watch TV upstairs tonight, okay?"

I looked at the opening credits on the screen and, sure enough, they were watching *End of Daze*. The credits seemed pretty creepy with their pulsing black type and a weird dry landscape in the background. "But I want to watch *this*."

"It's for grown-ups, sweetie." Dad reclined his armchair. "Why don't you watch one of your movies?"

"*Taylor*'s watching it." I put my hands on my hips.

Mom made a noise like a snort or tsk. It sounded like disapproval, whatever it was.

"I'm twelve years old!" I stood up taller.

Dad nodded. "Which is not quite old enough to watch this show." He jerked his head in the direction of the stairs. "Up. Now. We'll see you in the morning."

I stood there, trying to decide whether to go to battle over this, as my dad sipped his wine then put his glass down on a newspaper with a photo of a huge, lone cicada on the front page. The thing that everyone apparently found *so completely fascinating* about these cicadas was that they lived in the ground and only came out to make a big mess and mate every seventeen years. I already felt like I'd spent the last twelve years waiting—I wasn't even sure for what— and the idea that I might have to wait another five years for it made my skin jump and crawl.

But I wasn't sure I had it in me to fight about whether I was old enough to watch *End of Daze*. Not after having spent the last six months of school campaigning unsuccessfully for a cell phone and not after the day I'd had. So I said good night and went up to the office, where the other TV was, and moved some papers off the futon so that I could sit. I'd wanted this room to be mine when we'd moved in but the movers had put Mom's desk and sewing machine in there. She said we'd move them another time, but we hadn't yet, even though I still asked my parents like *every week* if I could switch rooms. I hated that my room was so far down the hall from theirs, like I was a guest in their house.

There was nothing worth watching on regular TV (the one downstairs was the only one with the good cable channels), and I had already seen all the movies we owned too many times. So I watched a half hour of nothing and then went to Mom's laptop to try to see if I could watch *End of Daze* online, but you couldn't unless you had a mobile/device login, which I was sure we didn't. My parents prided themselves on being "late adopters," which explained why I was the only person my age I knew who still didn't have a phone. So I snuck back downstairs and tiptoed to the door to the den. A mushroom cloud exploded on the screen. Plumes of dark smoke chased people around corners. The air itself seemed to be shaking.

Back in bed, I couldn't get the images out of my head and couldn't get to sleep. So I started playing Russia in my head.

Throw. Catch.

Throw. Bounce. Catch.

Throw. Bounce. Catch.

Throw. Clap. Clap. Clap. Catch.

Throw. Clap. Clap. Clap. Catch.

Throw . . . Clap . . . Catch . . .

It seemed no more or less dumb than counting sheep.

4.

There were still no cicadas in the morning, so I got dressed and told Mom I was going next door to get Taylor. But when I stepped outside, I saw Taylor's almost white-blonde hair—her parents had thought she was albino for a split-second when she was born—glinting in the morning sun . . . in front of Alyssa's house. They were playing Russia on the driveway.

"Hey," I called out as I crossed the street to join them. Then in a near-whisper I said to Taylor, "I thought we were going swimming."

Taylor looked at me blankly, and I felt my face get hot, like I was getting sunburned.

"Maybe later." Taylor spoke in an annoyed whisper.

Alyssa asked, "What are we doing later?"

"Nothing," I said.

"Going swimming at Julia's house," Taylor said.

How could she be so clueless?

"Oh." Alyssa bounced her ball. "I have a pool, too."

"Duh." I itched a pretend scratch on my neck, just for something to do. "We watched your whole house get built. We saw the pool being dug."

We all stood there and my mind drew a triangle with the three of us as the three points, and then Alyssa said, "Good for you, Julie."

"Julie-*ah*," I corrected.

Alyssa shrugged. "I like Julie better."

They went back to their bouncing and throwing.

"This game is dumb," I said.

Alyssa didn't even look at me. "Then don't play."

But I wasn't going to fall for that. I picked up a ball that had rolled to the curb and started at threesies, since that was the move they were on.

"You have to start at onesies." Alyssa pushed some hair out of her face.

"So, anyway, did you end up watching it?" Taylor asked her.

"Oh my god, it was so good!"

"I *know*!" Taylor nodded a few times, quickly. "Right?"

"Totally." Alyssa nodded, too, and I watched her move on to foursies, throwing the ball into air and circling her forearms around each other a few times like she was disco dancing, then catching the ball.

I threw the ball against the wall and caught it and struggled to push an ache in my jaw out of my mind. "That mushroom cloud was pretty scary," I said. "I think I had nightmares."

Alyssa laughed. "Fraidy cat!"

Taylor giggled, and the spinning motion of her hands on her fourth foursies move made me dizzy. But they were moving forward in the game, and it felt like learning how to play Russia was the only way I was going to be able to stick around. So I ignored the dizzies and paid superclose attention to everything Alyssa was doing. I learned how you had to throw the ball under your leg for fivesies and how you had to throw it under your arm and up in front of you for sixies. The game just seemed to go on and on . . . and I kept having to start it again and again.

Peter and Andrew skated over maybe an hour into it, right when Alyssa had reached thirteen for the first time all morning. I had to admit that the move for thirteen was super hard. You had to throw the ball then turn around then clap once in front, once in back, then again in front before catching it.

"What are you guys doing?" Peter tipped his skateboard up into his hand with his foot.

"It's called Russia," Alyssa said.

"Looks dumb," Peter said, and I wanted to run over and hug him. Peter was in my class at school—the smart kid class, but we weren't supposed to call it that—and was also in the band with me. When I watched him play trumpet, I sometimes daydreamed about holding hands or having my first kiss with him, but then he'd go and do something like talk about popping the wings off of cicadas—and how their heads would supposedly pop off, too—and the dream would go poof. He was wearing a JOE'S ICES shirt, which wasn't anything new since his father was Joe. Andrew wasn't in our class at school, just band (drums).

"Well, it isn't." Alyssa held her ball between her knees while she adjusted her ponytail. "It's really hard."

"Doesn't look hard," Peter said, and he and Andrew laughed.

"Two questions." Peter scrunched up his face as he watched Alyssa's ball go high. "Why's it called Russia? And who the heck are you?"

She didn't stop playing, didn't look at him when she said, "Alyssa. I live here now."

"That's only one answer," I said. "Why's it called Russia?"

"I don't know." Alyssa was on her fifth successful thirteensies move. I was pretty much in awe but didn't want to admit it. "My mom played it when she was a kid, like during the Cold War with Russia or something."

With Peter right there also thinking the game—and name—seemed dumb, I felt brave. "Cold War would be a better name," I said. "Russia's sort of stupid."

"Maybe it's you that's stupid," Alyssa said.

"Are you joking?" Peter hopped up onto his skateboard, and then spun around and hopped off. "Julia's like the smartest person in school. *And* the best clarinet player."

Alyssa caught the ball after her seventh or eighth thirteensies move she was doing; I was losing track. She said, "Then maybe you should make out with her."

I dropped my ball. I had nowhere else to look so I watched it roll and land in a small puddle by the curb. Taylor was laughing—Andrew, too. But then Peter said, "Maybe I will," and jumped onto his skateboard and pushed off down the block.

Andrew followed, shouting, "Later, gators."

I didn't care much about anything Alyssa or Taylor said after that—Peter might someday kiss me! He thought I was a good clarinet player!—and then a while later Mom called me home.

The two of us ate leftover pizza for lunch, and went out back and sat in the loungers on the deck. Lying there, the muscles in my arms ached from all that throwing. My neck hurt from looking up. I kept going over the moves in my head when Mom got a phone call and started saying things like, "Holy cow, do you remember?" and

"Stop, I'm going to hurt myself from laughing." I closed my eyes and wondered who she was talking to—probably my aunt Colleen, who wasn't really my aunt, just an old friend of Mom's—and wondered when Peter might get around to kissing me.

Would I be ready?

My parents were in front of the TV with wine in their glasses again when I came down after an after-dinner bath. "It's on *again*?"

"It's a two-night premiere," Dad said. "Before it switches to just Fridays."

Great. So I'd spend another night being an outcast in my own family. And now Taylor and Alyssa would have more new stuff to talk about that I knew nothing about. "*Please*, can I watch?" I pressed my hands together as if in prayer.

Dad sounded tired. "Julia, honey. We said no."

"But Taylor watched it. Alyssa, too." I could hear the whine in my voice but couldn't seem to replace it with a tone that was more reasonable, more mature.

"Oh, great." Mom reached for her wine. "Well, if *Alyssa* watches it!"

"Who's Alyssa?" Dad asked.

"The new girl," Mom said with some sharpness.

It was clear that that strategy was not going to work, that I'd have to find another way. "Well, can I at least go out in the yard for an hour? Maybe Peter's out with his telescope or something."

Maybe *Peter* could figure out how to get his hands on the show.

"Fine," Mom said. "But just for an hour. We're getting up early, and I'm not dragging you around the city all day if you're exhausted."

"Fine," I said.

"Look out for cicadas!" Dad said.

"I don't think they're coming at all." I opened the screen door.

Peter wasn't out stargazing—we shared a fence at the back of our yards—so I just sat for a while in one of the deck loungers and tried to pick out constellations.

Big Dipper.

Big deal.

I dreamed that I was being followed around the house by a buzzing, long-legged bug. I kept swatting it away but it kept coming back, all dangling and awful-looking, clicking in my face. I grabbed a glass from a kitchen cabinet and trapped the bug under it, on the countertop, where I studied its red eyes, its clear wings, its hard brown shell. I pulled a pen out of a drawer with an index card and labeled it, *Exhibit A*.

5.

Being a teacher was in my mom's blood so she couldn't shut it down on summer vacation. This trip to the city would probably involve a lesson in the history of skyscrapers or maybe the invention of plumbing. But it was a small price to pay for a shopping trip, and I was happy I'd have Taylor to share head-nodding duties.

I rang Taylor's bell Saturday morning, and she answered in her pajamas. "I can't go."

"What? Why not?"

"I don't feel good." She coughed, and I was sure it was fake. Something in the sound of it. Too shallow. Too dry.

"Oh."

I stopped myself from saying, *You were fine yesterday.*

"Yeah, well." She coughed again.

Again: fake.

I tried not to notice the way she kept looking over my shoulder, but I couldn't help it. I looked over toward Alyssa's house and saw some movement in an upstairs window.

"We'll go next Saturday instead!" I said. It was genius. "I'll go tell my mom!"

"No." Taylor shook her head and looked down. "You should go. You shouldn't let your mom down. We'll do something fun when I feel better."

I tried to think of fun things Taylor and I could do together, but I couldn't think fast enough.

Total blank.

"Okay," I said. "Sure." Then I made my way back to my house, where Mom had just started the car. I went to her window, which she opened when she saw me. "Taylor's sick."

"Huh." Mom cocked her head and slid her black sunglasses onto her face. "Well, that's too bad."

"Can we go another day?" I dared.

She looked in the rearview mirror and applied her lip gloss. "No, my dear." She smacked her lips. "We cannot."

I groaned and got in the car. Everything was falling apart and now I was stuck with Mom all day.

"Frankly"—she reached over and squeezed my knee—"I'm glad it's just the two of us."

I felt a pain in my gut as we pulled off the block, a fear of missing something or everything. I pictured Taylor and

Alyssa hanging out together all day, bonding over stuff like *End of Daze* and Russia.

The drive into the city was about an hour and Mom was quiet the whole time—which was a nice change. Lately it seemed like she was always asking questions about who I was with and what I was reading and what me and my friends were talking about and why wasn't I eating cookies anymore and on and on. So I just looked out the window, watching houses and warehouses and apartment buildings and Burger Kings and gas stations whir by. We went over a bridge that looked like it could take you straight up to heaven and took another highway to the tunnel.

I thought we'd never get there, with all the traffic, but then we turned into a parking garage and gave away the car keys. Soon we were in an elevator, going up to the way high top of one of the tallest buildings in the city. When Mom went to hold my hand in the elevator—too tight, as usual—I let her. It's not like anyone I knew was around to see.

We stepped out onto the observation deck and it was so bright that it really felt like we were closer to the sun. We walked around once and found a spot where we could just stand and take it all in. I saw tall apartment buildings with roof decks on them and wondered about the kind of people who lived so high up, who sat in those chairs at night as the city glistened around them. I looked at the cars way down, and pictured tiny people driving them. A sign near where we were standing said that visibility was fifteen miles in current conditions, but as the warm summer wind whipped against me, I caught my own reflection along with the city's in Mom's sunglasses and felt like I could see forever. I felt big and small and connected. I wasn't sure to what, but it was to something important.

After taking some pictures, we went back down, down, down, and walked a few blocks and went to lunch in a restaurant in the belly of a fancy department store. I had the best tuna sandwich of my life (though I had to pick some weird lettuce-type thing that was definitely not lettuce off it). Mom even ordered us fake cocktails. When they came, she raised a toast, "To mother-daughter day!"

I clinked my glass and it made a festive sound. I couldn't think of the last time I'd seen my mom so happy, so relaxed. And when I said, "Cheers!" I felt cheerful.

We shopped a little bit then. Mom bought some lip gloss, and I picked out a cool purse made of three kinds of neat metallic leather: silver, gold, and peach-tinted. I loved everything about it. The shine. The shape. The clean sound of the snap when it closed.

When we walked past the bedding department, I

thought about my own old spread at home. "Can we look around here?"

"Sure." Mom followed me into the displays of bedrooms, all fluffy and pretty and making me want to climb in.

"I came here when I needed stuff for my first apartment in the city." She ran a hand along a plaid bedspread that looked like it belonged in a country house. "It was such an exciting time." Then she sat on a bed with a big red flower at the center of the spread. "You have so many adventures ahead of you, Julia. You have no idea."

I wasn't sure how or why we'd gone from bedspreads to adventures, so I pointed at the bedspread. "Can I get it?" That red flower was calling me.

"Not now, honey." She looked at her watch. "We have to get going. And anyway, we should wait for a sale. But yes, we should get you a new bedspread."

"For my new room down the hall?" I tried.

She suddenly looked tired, like just being alive was too much work.

"I'll move the sewing machine myself!" I said. *"Please."*

"It's not that." She stood up and started to walk toward the elevators. "It's complicated, Julia."

"Why is it complicated?" I followed.

"Let me talk to your father." She hit the Down button.

"For real this time?"

"For real." She put an arm out against the elevator door

as I got in with a skip in my step. She was going to talk to Dad about the room; this was real progress. So as we made our way back to the parking garage, I didn't even mind talking to her about the book I was reading. It was an old paperback called *The Haunted Pond* that I'd found at a garage sale a week ago—about a girl and a crippled boy who discover a haunted pond where a mysterious face sometimes appeared.

"Sounds a little creepy," she said. "And 'cripple' isn't really a word that people use anymore."

"They use it in the book. And I *like* creepy things." It seemed like a good idea to start building a case for why I should be allowed to watch the rest of *End of Daze*.

"Why?" Mom asked. "Like what specifically do you like about the story?"

"Mom!" She sure knew how to kill a mood. "I'm not writing a book report. I just like it. Okay?"

"Okay," she said. "Sorry. For being *interested in my own daughter*." She pinched me softly on the arm and I smiled. She had a point, I guessed.

Alyssa and Taylor were playing Russia in front of Taylor's house when we turned onto the block. They each had a ball and they were throwing them into the air and clapping under their legs and turning.

Over and over.

My mind was blanking on which number move it was.

As we pulled into our driveway, Taylor dropped her ball and had to run into the street to get it. She waved weakly when we got out of the car, but I focused on Alyssa, who was smiling but also trying not to.

"Can I go over?" I asked Mom. I wanted to show off my new purse.

"No," she said. "Your father made dinner."

It was Alyssa who called out to us. "Taylor's feeling a lot better!"

Mom waved and said, "A miraculous recovery!"

She turned to me, and my reflection was still there in her sunglasses, but no longer sparkling and deep.

"Come on, Julia." She put an arm around my shoulder, and I had to fight not to squirm free. "Let's go inside."

The kitchen was full of heat and strange smells.

"Ladies!" Dad was shaking a frying pan around over the stove. "How was your big day?"

Mom went over and kissed him after he put the pan down. He wiped his hands on a dish towel.

"We had the best time," she gushed, turning to me. "Didn't we?"

"It was great." But already I felt the magic of the day wearing away.

There were mushrooms in the pan.

I hated mushrooms.

My parents didn't care.

"Wait." Dad furrowed his brow. "Wasn't Taylor supposed to go with you? She was out with that new girl all day."

More magic going poof.

So Mom explained about what she called the "sudden onset" of Taylor's "mysterious illness." We sat down for dinner, but I just pushed my food around the plate, unable to eat. When I realized that Mom had noticed, I took a few bites, forcing food down with slugs of cold water. I knew I was spoiling our day by letting it be spoiled by Taylor and Alyssa, and I felt bad, but I couldn't think of anything to do about it.

After I helped clean up, I went out to the yard with a tennis ball and started to play Russia alone. I was only up to fivesies when Peter called out to me from his yard. "Hey," he said.

"Hey, yourself."

"How are you doing?"

I could see his red shirt through slits in the fence. "I'm miserable," I said. "How are *you* doing?"

"I'm okay, I guess. Why miserable? I heard you went into the city today, so that sounds pretty nonmiserable."

I sighed. "It was fun. But I don't know." For a second I was afraid to say it. But this was Peter, so I went for it. "The new girl? Alyssa?"

He nodded.

"She's kind of mean to me. And she's stealing Taylor away."

"What do you care? You have Wendy." Wendy James was my best friend from school. She was a little bit overweight and sometimes had dandruff and I hadn't seen or talked to her since school let out. "Isn't she your best friend?"

"No, Taylor is," I said. She was a lot cooler than Wendy. "But now Alyssa is pushing us apart."

I could see one of Peter's eyes now, peeking through the biggest slit, the slit we always talked through. He said, "She's kind of mean to me, too."

"It's different." I tried to bounce my ball on the grass, and it landed with a *thud* in my vegetable garden.

"If you say so," he said.

I bent down and found the ball under a tomato plant; I really needed to weed. But not now. "Hey, are you watching *End of Daze*?"

"Nah," he said through the slit. "Not allowed."

"*Stiiinks,*" I said.

"What's the big deal?"

"Everyone's watching it but me."

"And me!"

"And you." It didn't make me feel any better, though. "My parents aren't even taping it. If they were DVRing it, I could at least try to sneak it. But they're watching it when it's on, like clockwork. So annoying."

"Is it online?" he asked.

"You need some special login for that channel for devices or something."

"I'll see what I can do," he said, and my heart filled with hope.

Inside, my parents were side by side on the couch, talking quietly, and I thought about the stories they used to tell me about myself as a toddler, how I'd see them snuggling on the couch or curled up in bed and I'd push in between them, whining, "I wanna cuddle, too!" I wasn't sure I'd ever been able to kick the feeling of being lonely in their company, and I sometimes wondered whether everybody felt like that around them, since they were so obviously in love, or if it was just me.

They looked up at the same time, as if surprised to see me, and Mom adjusted her position, moving closer to Dad, who yawned.

"You want to play Bananagrams or something?" she asked, but I didn't have the heart to make them move, not one inch.

Up in my room, pajamas on, I thought about reading, which usually made me happy, but tonight I didn't think it would. I pulled the monkey Peter had given me into bed, snuggling close.

6.

"It's too bad about yesterday," I said when I went over to Taylor's the next morning. Mom had woken me up early and dragged me to Mass, so I was home and changed into shorts by ten thirty.

"Yeah, well." Taylor was sitting on her front stoop, looking over toward Alyssa's. Not reading a book or anything. Just sitting there.

"At least you're feeling better." I couldn't look her in the eye so I watched an ant that was marching across one of the bricks of her front steps and wondered whether ants got jealous during the cicada years. It was funny to think about them getting miffed about the cicadas getting all that press when it was true every second of every day of *every year* that ants could do amazing things like carry something twenty times their own body weight.

"That was some weird flu or something, right?" I heard my own forced laugh as the ant disappeared into a crack. "Like a two-minute bug or something?"

"What are you even talking about?" Taylor snapped.

"I just mean you got better fast is all." My face heated up again.

"Yeah, I did." She huffed. "So why are you making such a big deal out of it?"

I didn't know.

"Look what I got." I held out my purse, which now held my wallet, some lip balm, and my book. I thought about telling Taylor all about *The Haunted Pond*, but then I didn't.

"It's nice," Taylor said, but she sounded sort of sad and I wondered if maybe she was jealous. I hoped so. I hoped she regretted not coming because maybe she could have bought something awesome, too.

"Why don't we play Spit or go swimming?" I said. "Just the two of us. My dad's talking about covering the pool for a few days because of the cicadas, so this might be our last chance all week."

"I'm just going to hang out." Taylor put her elbows on her knees.

"Okay, then." I sat down next to her. "I'll hang out, too."

She looked at me funny for a long moment. "You're suffocating me."

"What?" This was weird.

"I only mean it's, you know, good to have other friends." She adjusted her ponytail. "We should both have other friends."

"Well, duh. Of course." I felt instantly like I might be coming down with some weird, sudden bug, too. "But I don't know. Why do you even like her?"

"I just do, okay?"

"She's mean to me." I blurted. Maybe telling Peter had given me confidence.

"She's not *mean*." Taylor sighed. "She's just, I don't know . . . she's funny. And here she is!"

Alyssa had appeared at the base of the driveway, bouncing her ball. She had gum in her mouth, and it made me think of something my mom said all the time, claiming it was something *her mom* used to say. *What are you, a cow? Chewing cud?* I wasn't even sure what cud was but I was still tempted to say it.

"My mom's at the mall for like an hour," Alyssa said. "Let's go to my house."

Taylor stood up, but I didn't. "I'm not sure I'm allowed," I said. My parents only ever left me home alone when they went out to get pizza or making a quick trip to the bank or drugstore.

"Well, *we're* going." Alyssa shrugged and walked off, and Taylor copied her shrug and followed.

It was only across the street. My parents wouldn't even have to know and they were probably too busy cuddling on the couch to care, anyway. Weekends were all about the cuddling for those two.

There were no cars in Alyssa's driveway, and the house was quiet except for the hum of the refrigerator. She led us through the kitchen, up the stairs, and into a room where a bunch of boxes sat untouched. The carpet was beige and really soft, and the walls were all clean and white. It smelled like new house, and there was a Ouija board in the middle of the floor.

"This is all my grandmother's stuff." Alyssa sat down in front of the Ouija board. "We're going to try to talk to her."

"No way," I said.

"What, are you afraid of *everything*?" Alyssa said.

"No, it's just. I don't know."

But I *did* know. "Praying to dead people is one thing, because you're not expecting them to talk back, but expecting an answer seems wrong."

"Oh my god," Alyssa said. "You *pray*?"

It was pretty funny that she'd said *Oh my god* while asking me that question.

So what if I did?

That was one thing. This was another.

I said, "I seriously doubt that dead people are waiting

around for their relatives to pull out a Ouija board so they can talk."

Taylor was sitting cross-legged across from Alyssa. She turned and said, "So leave," with a shrug.

These two could really shrug.

I sat down and let my fingers rest lightly on the gliding piece alongside theirs and felt a surge of anger, like I suddenly had too much blood in my body and it was trying to get out any which way, pressing on me from the inside out.

Alyssa took a deep breath and exhaled. "Okay, everybody close your eyes."

She did, and then Taylor did. So I did, too.

"We are here today," Alyssa said, all serious, "to try to talk to my grandmother, Camille. Will you let us know if you are in the room with us, Grandma?"

Beneath my fingers I felt the piece jitter. It slid across the board a bit and then more and then stopped. When I opened my eyes, the window with the needle in it was pointing to the word YES.

"Holy cow," Taylor said. "I just got chills."

But I wasn't buying it.

Alyssa said, "Grandma? I want you to tell me, if you can, where the money is. I know you had cash that you packed. Can you tell me where it is?"

The piece started to move under my fingers, hitting

letters one by one. The answer, when complete, spelled out TOWELS.

"What does it mean?" Taylor's eyes got big.

"There." Alyssa got up and walked across the room to some boxes. "This one," she said. Sure enough the box was labeled TOWELS.

She ripped the top open. Taylor rushed to her side, and I did, too, and then there was Alyssa, holding an envelope full of cash.

I seriously thought I might faint or something. "Now *I* just got chills."

Because it had actually *worked*!

Alyssa and Taylor busted out laughing.

Alyssa stopped long enough to say, "You are so gullible."

"We totally got you!" Taylor squealed.

"Yeah." I just waited a second for the inside-out pressure to stop again. "You really got me good."

"Come here." Alyssa got up. "I want to show you something."

She went to the window that faced the back of the house—there were no drapes or blinds—and pointed toward the house behind hers. "See that window there with the red curtains?"

"Yeah?" Taylor said.

"There's a couple that lives there, and sometimes they walk around naked."

"No way!" Taylor laughed.

I wanted to head for the stairs and pretend I'd never come here with them.

"The guy's pretty hairy and gross," Alyssa said. "The girl's all right, but she needs a boob job."

Taylor shook her head. "You are too much."

I might have imagined it or it might have actually been true, but I heard Mom's voice calling me home, so I said, "I think my mom's calling me."

"Well, go on home to Mommy then." Alyssa shooed me with her hand.

I turned to Taylor. "I left my purse on your porch."

"That's yours?" Alyssa was back at the Ouija board. She said, "Is Julia's new purse nice?" And she pushed the sliding piece over to the word NO.

"Just go get it, Julia." Taylor really seemed to want me gone. "You know where it is."

7.

"Where's Taylor?" Mom asked. She and Dad were sitting side by side at the kitchen table looking at something on Mom's laptop. No one had been calling for me at all.

"Oh," I said. "She's busy."

I felt awkward in my own body. I had no idea what to do with my arms, and wanted to ask Mom some questions about the birds and the bees and boob jobs. But it felt too weird now that I had the image of a hairy man in my brain. And anyway, Dad was there.

"Do you have the receipt for my purse?" I asked.

"I don't know, why?" Mom was only half paying attention. "Is something wrong with it?"

I looked at it, thinking I'd try to find something defective about it, but I still liked it. I sure liked it better than Alyssa's tacky chair and her ridiculous stuffed giraffe. "Never mind. So did you ask him?"

Now Mom looked up. "Ask who what?"

"Dad." I turned to him. "Can I *please-please-please* move into the office?"

He was about to say something, but Mom cut him off.

"Julia. I want to talk to your dad about that privately, okay?"

He squeezed her shoulder.

I went upstairs and thought about reading, but instead changed into my swimsuit. I went out to the pool and sat down at the edge, with my feet in, waiting for a face to appear so I wouldn't be alone. I was also hoping to get hot—hot enough to want to dive right in—but there was too much shade, so I moved to a lounge chair and closed my eyes and tried to sleep, but I wasn't tired.

Then Peter called out "Julia," and I looked up and saw movement—blue shirt today—behind the fence. I walked over, and Peter said, "Meet me in the woods in ten minutes?"

"Okay!"

I ran through the house, shouting out that I was going over to Peter's.

Since we'd had woods by our old house, I'd been excited when Peter had first shown me the woods across the street from him. Even better, these woods had a pond—not haunted—that we could ice-skate on. This past winter a big branch had fallen and frozen into it in just

the right spot for jumps. We sat on that same branch now—
the part that was on dry land—with Peter's dad's iPad.

"It took me a while to figure out the password," Peter
said, "but we're good to go."

It felt wrong to be watching a television show in the
woods—and also wrong to be watching *End of Daze*
against my parents' orders—but it was also thrilling in a
butterflies-in-stomach way. They weren't going to be
able to keep me from growing up no matter how hard they
tried, and this was hardly the worst way for me to start.

The trees offered just enough shade that we could see
the images on the screen without too much glare, and I
swear it was like neither of us moved the whole time, not for
a whole hour or whatever an hour without commercials was.

I saw the scenes I'd glimpsed that first night—of the
mushroom cloud, of people being chased around corners
by smoke. But now I learned the names of the main
characters—Mack and Archer—a father and son who survived
a chemical bomb attack on New York because they'd
retreated to their crazy neighbor Buddy's underground
bunker. They were freaking out because Archer wanted
his mom, but she was at work and also probably dead, and
Mack and Buddy agreed they couldn't go out for a few
days. Buddy had an old radio but the news was grim—
attacks in Europe, China, all across the US. And then the
broadcast stopped all together. Eventually, the three of

them left the bunker and started roaming the streets of the city, looking for food and water. But there were bodies everywhere, and Buddy started to get crazier, and he threatened Mack and, well, Mack had to take him out. Together, Mack and Archer made their way across town to the office where Helen, the mom, worked, and they found her body among the dead. The hour ended with them both weeping over her body : . . and then her cell phone rang. Mack picked it up and said, "Hello?"

Roll credits.

"Oh, come on!" Peter shouted.

"Wow." My butt was killing me.

Peter got up and stretched. "I thought there were going to be zombies."

I straightened my legs out in front of me, shifted my bones. "You sound disappointed."

He bent and picked up a stick. "Zombies are cool."

"Do you think that could really happen?" I asked.

He poked a lily pad on the pond with his stick. "Doubt it."

I watched as a few tiny fish, probably annoyed by that stick, swam away from us. "But the world can't last forever."

"It's done all right so far," Peter said. "I mean, if you ignore the whole global warming fiasco that our species has brought about by its self-serving lifestyle."

I smiled. I liked the way Peter talked.

We tried to skip stones for a few minutes, but the pond was too shallow. I looked up at the trees. "Do you really think these cicadas are coming?"

"Oh, they're just days away." Peter tried to land a small stone on a lily pad a few times but failed.

"I'll believe it when I see it." I liked not caring about something that everyone else was so caught up in.

"Come here." He picked his stick up again and walked over to a tree a little bit farther into the woods and crouched down.

I followed.

"Look." Peter pointed to all these weird little holes in the ground at the base of the tree. "They're going to climb out of these."

"Gross."

"Not gross. Cool. If they're tunneling up, it means the ground temp has finally hit sixty-two."

"You're such a boy." I stood up and put some distance between me and those holes.

"You're such a girl." Now it was my sneaker he poked with a stick.

"I thought I found an old treasure map right here once," Peter said.

"Really?" We started to make our way back out of the woods on the path, me first.

"Yeah, there was this box I dug up that had old Native

American coins in it and an old map with a chest of gold marked with an *X* and some small broken colored glass bottles, like for perfume or something."

"Awesome." I pushed a branch out of my way, and turned to hold it for Peter.

"Not awesome. It turns out my brother had planted it there." He slipped past the branch and past me. "It was a joke. I was *crushed*."

I took a minute to think about that, how exciting and awful it would all have been. "I would've been, too."

Just before we reached the street, a yellow butterfly flew over a small patch of purple wildflowers. I imagined it was one of the butterflies that had been in my stomach while I was going against my parents' orders, and that it had somehow gotten free—and freed me. And as I watched Peter step out into the grass that separated woods from his street, and I saw the sun light up his hair, I knew I now officially had a crush on him. And in spite of Alyssa and Russia and Mack and Archer, I felt for a moment like everything was pretty great.

I said a quick prayer—whatever, Alyssa—that the world wouldn't end while I was still on it, and definitely not before I'd been kissed by Peter.

8.

"So are there any cute boys around here?" Alyssa
said from a lounge chair on my back deck the next day. I'd
wanted to sit there—it was *my* chair, *my* favorite—but I
felt silly saying so. "In my old neighborhood there were cute
boys everywhere."

I had spent a good part of the morning thinking
about Peter, imagining us in scenes like some of the ones
in *The Haunted Pond*, all dramatic and tense. We were
going to watch the second episode of *End of Daze* tomorrow
morning if he could get the iPad and we could both get
away. The plan was to meet in the woods at ten, and if one
of us didn't show, abandon mission. It all felt secretive in
the best way possible.

"There's just Peter and Andrew, and they're not that

cute," Taylor said, which was a change of tune but then I realized she *had* pretty much stopped flirting with Andrew. It was true he'd never really flirted back.

I said, "Peter totally is," before realizing I probably didn't want Alyssa knowing who I thought was cute. Because if Alyssa decided to like Peter, I'd be so mad. And worse, what if he actually liked *her*? Maybe she was mean to him because she liked him. Maybe he actually liked it? Maybe he'd only kiss me if he couldn't kiss her instead.

"Yeah, if you like band geeks." Taylor looked at Alyssa, who smiled approval.

I was so beyond mad that we had even ended up here in my backyard. It was exactly the scenario I'd been putting all of my energy into preventing. I thought if I could spend enough solo time with Taylor, Alyssa would never really compete. But when I called Taylor in the morning to get to her first and invite her over, she'd said she'd love to ". . . if Alyssa can come, too."

How could she not know that that was like the rudest thing in the world? How could I say no without seeming like I was doing more suffocating?

I'd made a fist while saying, "Sure, of course!" in the sweetest tone I could manage.

So here we were.

Alyssa had brought some magazines of her mom's, and they were both flipping through them. I reached for the sunscreen on the table next to my chair.

"I think it's a little late for that," Alyssa said.

I studied the white lotion in my palm, and had a quick thought about clowns and pies. Specifically the ways clowns smash pies into people's faces. I said, "What are you talking about?"

"I just mean you already look like a tomato." She turned a page. "A freckled tomato."

"Alyssa," Taylor said, like it was a warning.

So Alyssa *was* mean! Even Taylor thought so!

"What?" Alyssa sniffed a perfume sample in her magazine. "It's true."

"But you don't *say* it!" Taylor shook her head, but she was smiling.

I put the sunscreen tube down. "At least I won't get cancer."

"I don't burn; I tan." Alyssa closed her eyes and looked up at the sun.

"Doesn't matter." I rubbed in my lotion. "You can still get cancer. Tell her, Taylor."

Taylor's grandfather had to have a chemical peel on his nose because of skin cancer. And he was Italian and dark-skinned. We'd both been horrified when he turned up at her family's Memorial Day barbecue with his face practically falling off.

"Chill out, Julia." Taylor shook her head. "It's just a little tan."

"Your grandfather's *nose* practically fell off!"

"He's old," Taylor said.

I put my sunglasses on to hide my eyes. I tried to talk myself through a game of Russia in my mind as a distraction.

Throw, catch.

Throw, bounce, catch.

Throw, bounce, catch.

Throw, clap, clap, clap, catch.

And on and on . . .

Mom came out of the house a few minutes later with a pitcher of lemonade and some polka-dot plastic cups. Her freckles were even worse than mine, and I felt horribly embarrassed of her in her tank top and shorts that showed so much of her skin. Freckles everywhere.

"I thought you girls might like some lemonade," she said.

Alyssa smiled real wide and said, "Thanks, Mrs. Richards." I didn't even know how she knew my last name. "That's so sweet of you."

Mom raised her eyebrows at Alyssa. "Well, aren't you polite." She poured a glass and handed it to Alyssa, and I could see that Mom was reading the headlines on the magazine on the table. One of them was, TEN MOVES THAT WILL DRIVE HIM CRAZY.

"I hope you're wearing sunscreen," she said to Alyssa.

Alyssa sat up straighter, like she was offended. "Of course I am."

Taylor snickered when my mom was gone. "You're unbelievable," she said to Alyssa.

An hour later, when we got tired of swimming and lounging, Taylor suggested we go hang out in my room. I tried and tried to talk them out of it but there was no escaping—Alyssa said she really wanted to see it—and then there we were, standing in front of my unicorn poster.

"So are you *sure* you don't believe in unicorns?" Alyssa giggled.

"Oh," I said. "That old thing?"

With Alyssa in my room, everything looked unbearably babyish. I wanted to cut my flowery bedspread to pieces and shatter the carousel on my shelf before Alyssa could spot it, but then she did.

"*How* old are you?" Alyssa snorted, and Taylor laughed.

While they were looking at the clothes in my closet, I swept the Snow White and the Seven Dwarfs figures on my dresser into a drawer in a panic. Dopey hit his head on the drawer edge too hard, and cracked into pieces. I gasped.

"What happened?" Taylor asked.

I closed the drawer. "Oh, nothing."

I took down a photo of me and Wendy that had been stuck in the edge of my mirror and slipped it into the same drawer. If Alyssa got a look at her, I'd never live it down.

"Julia, my dear," she said. "Your room is in serious need of a makeover."

"Well, I haven't done anything in here because I'm moving down the hall."

Taylor sat on the bed. "Since when?"

"Since this weekend," I said. "Me and my mom looked at bedspreads and stuff when we were in the city. It's going to be awesome."

My mom called out from downstairs. "Girls! Sorry, but it's time to go home."

It was still only midafternoon. If they left, I knew they'd probably just go to one of their houses and hang out some more without me. And the more often they did that, the more I was sunk. "But Mom!" I yelled out.

"Sorry! Time to go!" Her voice may have sounded normal to Taylor and Alyssa but not to me. So I showed them to the door and stormed into the kitchen. "Why did you make them leave?"

"I need help with dinner."

But she didn't look like she needed help with dinner. She was reading the newspaper, and dinner wasn't for at least two hours.

I turned and looked at her and was about to say something about how she was ruining my life, but then I felt this feeling of relief come over me, like someone had pulled a plug on my feet and tension could just drain out through my toes. I was glad they were gone. I had to work so hard all the time when they were around.

Mom flipped a page in her paper and sighed. "What can I say"—she shook her head—"I don't like her."

She pushed the paper aside. "And you, dear daughter, are not going to spend your whole summer throwing a ball around and reading trashy magazines. I've signed you up for a music day camp starting next Monday. For two weeks."

"What?" I felt that fist form again. If I was off the block for two weeks, I'd never be able to keep Taylor on my side. "You can't do that!"

"I can. And I did."

"You're ruining everything," I said, now that it was officially true.

"Yeah, well," she said. "Sometime that's my job."

"Well, what did you decide about the room?" That would be at least one good thing that was happening to make my life not entirely miserable. "Can I move, at least?"

Her shoulders drooped. "Honey, we're going to need to hold off on that right now. But we can certainly spruce your room up a bit."

"But I *just* told my friends it was happening."

"That wasn't very smart of you." She got up and dumped her water into the kitchen sink and refilled it with newer, colder water. "And what do *they* care, anyway?"

"You don't even use that office!" I shouted. "Ever!"

She put her glass down and just stood there, looking

out the kitchen sink window. Her voice was deep when she said, "Go to your room."

I stormed upstairs and took the unicorn down off the wall, rolled it, and shoved it in the back of my closet. I flipped over my flower bedspread to the solid green side and put the stuffed monkey in a drawer with some winter sweaters that I couldn't imagine ever needing to wear again.

I put the carousel in the closet, too, and declared war on some old mermaid decals on the wall. But when I tried to peel one off, it ripped, leaving a mermaid amputee behind. I groaned and flopped down on the bed, where I was left looking up at a shelf that held a whole row of glassy-eyed dolls—dolls!—each of them dressed in the traditional garb of their country of origin. I wanted to box them up and send them all back to where they'd come from.

I wanted to get rid of everything.

The problem was this: I had nothing to put in its place.

I played Russia in the backyard after dinner and wished Peter would come out but he didn't. After a while, Dad came out with a beer, sat in a lounger, and said, "What on *earth* are you doing?"

"It's a game," I said. "It's called Russia."

"Why's it called that?" He snapped the can open.

"Some Cold War thing from the eighties or something?" I was on sevensies, so I dribbled the ball seven times, hit it toward the side of the house, and caught it.

"Fascinating," he said.

"Do you remember it? The Cold War?" I wasn't really sure what it was.

"I was young, but yes." He put the beer down beside his chair. "What do you want to know?"

"Well," I said. "What *was* it?"

He sighed. "It was basically years and years of conflict and tension between Russia and the US. You've heard of the Cuban Missile Crisis, right?"

"Uh, not really."

"That was the peak of it." He relaxed back into the chair. "Basically, we—the US—tried to overthrow the government of Cuba and failed. And then Russia offered to put missiles in Cuba so that we could never do that again, and the whole thing escalated into a situation where everyone thought we were headed for nuclear war. Total mutual destruction."

"Yikes." I was moving on to eights.

"Yeah. But mostly it was everybody making veiled threats, nobody really wanting to confront each other for real. A ton of psychological game playing and power grabs."

"Sounds like my life right now."

He sipped his beer. "That bad?"

I didn't want to get into it with him—the Alyssa-Taylor Crisis—so I just said, "Mom signed me up for camp without even asking me. Sounds like a power grab to me."

I threw and caught my fourth of eight, but I was losing interest in the game.

"I'm sure she thinks it's what's best for you," Dad said. "And she is, you may have noticed, often right."

"But why won't she let me have her office?" I threw the ball against the house and caught it.

"It's complicated, Julia." He sat up, straddling the lounger. "But I'm working on it, okay?"

What could be so complicated about it?

"Don't stay out too late." Dad got up. "Your mom wants to say good night."

He drifted in to watch TV, and I went up to say good night to Mom, who was going along with my strategy of pretending we hadn't had that fight that afternoon, and went to my room. I climbed into bed with my book, which was starting to get *really* good, especially now that one of my main daydreams was that my parents would send me away to live with some relative I'd never heard of, where I'd meet some tragic boy who saw ghosts in the pond in the backyard and who also just happened to be Peter.

I read page after page after page, grateful that the book pushed out the bouncing balls of Russia—and thoughts about the inevitable end of the world—for a while.

Girl.

Cripple.

Haunted pond.

Kiss and catch.

Peter.

9.

When I asked Mom if I could go over to Peter's on
Tuesday morning, to find out if he was going to band camp
and to see if he maybe wanted to play Wii in his basement
for a while, she said sure—like it was the best idea she'd ever
heard. So I went around the corner to meet him in the
woods. He was waiting, right on the same log where we'd
watched episode one, so I took a seat beside him. I realized
that I had a ball in my hand, and I put it on the ground beside
me. We'd barely started the show before we heard voices.

Girls' voices.

Taylor's and Alyssa's.

When they appeared by the pond, Peter and I froze.

"Well, looky looky," Alyssa said. "What are you two
lovebirds doing?"

"Shut up, Alyssa." I couldn't believe she was here in the woods, mine and Peter's.

"Good comeback." She swatted at a bug that may or may not have been a cicada.

"Does your mom know you're here?" Taylor asked.

Andrew arrived behind them. "Wait up, guys!"

"What do you care?" I picked up my ball, preparing to leave. I would have given my left arm for a unicorn to appear in the woods just then, to prove Alyssa wrong about something, anything.

"She thinks she's such a badass," Alyssa said, and Taylor laughed.

And I thought about my tomato face and those circus clowns and I threw my ball at Alyssa.

At Alyssa's hideous face.

Hard.

She screamed.

"How did you get to be so *mean*?" I said, and the last word came out as my own sort of scream. My throat hurt from it.

Alyssa's hands were covering her face and when she pulled them away she was all red—like sunburned. "I had no idea you were such a . . ."

Birds took off—a full flock by the sound of it—right as she called me the very word I'd been calling her in my mind since meeting her. We all heard it. Even with all that squawking and flapping.

"Oh, man," Andrew said. "I'm outta here."

Peter looked at him and looked dazed for a minute as Andrew took off down the path. Then Taylor took Alyssa's arm and calmly said, "Come to my house. You need ice."

I took off running toward home—Peter called out, "Julia, wait!"—and went straight to my room and buried my face in my pillow and cried.

How dare she call me that?

A minute later, I got up, wiped away tears and turned on the air conditioner in the window, even though Dad said never to run it during the day. I lay back down, took a few deep breaths, and decided to read. The girl and the crippled boy were sitting by the pond together, and a storm was brewing in the skies above them, and I got the sense that it was all building toward some big event. Like a kiss or a declaration of love or a horrible disfiguring accident.

But all of a sudden I didn't want the book to end—it was the only thing I had to truly look forward to—so I put it down and closed my eyes and imagined that it was *me* who was the victim of some horrible disfiguring accident. And that it was all somehow Alyssa's fault. And how sorry Taylor would be for not being nicer to me and how she'd be my best friend again and tell Alyssa to buzz off. Everyone would hate Alyssa at school, where I'd walk the halls like a war hero. I wouldn't be able to play Russia anymore because of my injuries and everyone would think that was horribly tragic.

My door opened.

Mom, of course. "Are you sick?"

"No." I rolled to my side away from her and could almost feel my imaginary wounds in my bones.

"Then what are you doing?"

"I'm relaxing. Can't I ever just relax?" I rolled my eyes before closing them again.

"Yes. For ten more minutes. Then I want to hear the sweet sound of your clarinet wafting down the hall."

"Mo-om!" I noted the exact time on the clock.

"I'm serious." She closed the door but came back a second later and turned off the air conditioner.

I got up exactly eleven minutes later and pulled my clarinet case out of my closet and sat with it on the bed. The smell that came out when I opened it wasn't entirely pleasant. And something about it—some weird combination of cork wax and old spit and wood—made me feel sad.

I popped a reed into my mouth to get it wet while I put the four pieces of the instrument together, and slipped the reed into its holder and screwed it into place. Resting the clarinet on the bed, I set up my music stand and pulled out some music from the school concert last year. I selected the *Swan Lake* Ballet Suite, op. 20: Scene, picked up my clarinet, and started to play.

I was hot.

I opened a window.

The curtains shifted a little, so there was at least a tiny breeze. I heard balls bouncing, and voices. Alyssa and Taylor were back at it, back at Russia.

I didn't care.

I just played the piece the whole way through and noticed for the first time how it started off sad, then got angry, then got strong, and I imagined the sound of a concert band around me as I carried the melody.

I played it again, and it sounded better that time.

After one more run through that was almost perfect, I went downstairs and made a snack, melting fake cheese onto nachos and dipping them in salsa. When I burned my tongue, it sort of felt good.

It started at the tail end of dinner. Right as we were finishing up our last bits of meatloaf, mashed potatoes, and carrots, the phone rang. And when Mom picked up, no one was there.

"That's weird," she said, sitting back down.

Almost immediately, the phone rang again, and this time *I* picked it up. Somebody—a girl—said something in Spanish or maybe Italian or maybe just gibberish. I wasn't sure I recognized the voice. I hung up. Then I asked to be excused.

Mom came to my room again a while later, after the phone rang downstairs for the last time. From my bed, I had heard her picking it up a bunch of times, answering with increasing bite, before giving up and calling out, "I'm unplugging it!"

I knew it had to be Alyssa.

"Anything you want to talk about?" Mom asked, sitting on the foot of my bed.

"Not really." I pictured the red spot that had immediately formed on Alyssa's face where the ball had hit.

Mom was looking around my room, and it was like she couldn't figure out what was different. She cleared some wrinkles in the bedspread with a flat palm. "Any idea who's calling?"

I couldn't make myself lie and I felt like I might start to cry.

So I told her.

About everything that had been going on since Alyssa had moved to the block.

How she made fun of my clothes, my room.

What she'd said about my freckles and to Peter.

About the Ouija board and the money and the peep show.

How *mean* she was.

How Taylor didn't seem to care and said I was suffocating her.

How I felt like *I* was suffocating.

Then I told her about the ball I threw at Alyssa's hideous face.

"Oh, Julia." Her sigh sounded like disappointment.

And if it was true that I'd let her down, then I was really done for.

So I lost it.

Full-on sobbing meltdown.

Mom went to get me tissues. I tried to clean up, but she pulled me into a hug and even though I didn't want *her* to hug me, I wanted to be hugged.

"They're not worth it, honey," she said, pulling back after a minute. "People who make you this upset, who say things like that? They're not real friends."

"But Taylor's my *best friend*!"

She looked a little crazed then, in her eyes, and it scared me a little. Like I'd made a big mistake bringing her into this. "Is she?"

"Of course she is." I wiped my nose.

She huffed and seemed to literally bite her tongue. "Is this how best friends treat each other?"

I didn't want to hear anything she was saying. Taylor

had to be my best friend. Because if not her, then who? Wendy? No way. Apart from that time when I stashed her photo in a drawer, I hadn't really thought about her since school let out. Didn't that mean something? That I didn't miss her? It had to.

"Why doesn't she like me?" I asked. "Alyssa, I mean."

Mom shook her head. "You can't do anything about whether people like you or not. Except the obvious things, like not being mean or intentionally hurting someone."

It sounded like a question. "I'm not! I didn't!"

"Okay then," she said.

"But what am I going to do?"

"You're going to think about the fact that maybe *you* don't like *her*." She stood and went to my mirror, pushed her hair behind her ears and studied herself. "Maybe you don't even really like Taylor all that much either."

"Of course I do!" I shouted.

But I wasn't so sure anymore, not after the way she'd been siding with Alyssa so much. Thinking back on how things used to be, it was hard to believe that Taylor was still the same person I'd had sleepovers with over winter break, and told all my secrets, like how I once tried to practice kissing using my own hand. It wasn't that simple, though. "They live on our *street*."

She nodded. "And I don't really like Mrs. Chamberlain, but we still live on the same street and are civil and don't pretend we're anything more than neighbors. I'm not really friends with Taylor's mom, either. I mean I help her out with Taylor when she has work stuff and she's helped me, too, but it's not like we talk about important things."

It was true that Mom *really* didn't like Mrs. Chamberlain, who was also saying weird things about our house or yard, like "I see you're going for the wild look with the lawn!" It was also true that Mom and Taylor's mother never really spoke for more than a few minutes. It was always just about us girls, or stuff happening on the block.

"Why *aren't* you friends with Taylor's mom?"

She looked caught out in her reflection in the mirror. "We just don't have a lot in common." She untucked her hair from her ears and turned back to me. "When you start school again it won't matter as much as it does now."

"But summer's another five weeks!"

"Well, you'll have camp starting next week." She seemed ready to be done with this conversation; I felt the same. "This week, why don't you have Wendy over?"

I would not invite Wendy over if I could avoid it. "Maybe."

We went downstairs, and I helped her clean up dinner. When we were done, she walked over to the phone and plugged it back in. It started ringing before she'd even let go of the wire.

"That's it," she snapped. "I've had it."

She opened and closed a few kitchen drawers. She

pulled something out of the back of the junk drawer—a
whistle I'd gotten in a birthday goodie bag a few years
ago—and propped it by her lips. Picking up the phone mid-
ring, she blew that whistle so hard—it was louder than
that whole party had been—that her face turned red. I
covered my ears.

"What on earth?" Dad said from the other room.

"Come on." Mom unplugged the phone again, grabbed
her car keys off the hook on the wall, and called out to
Dad. "We're going out for dessert. You want to come?"

I could hear baseball coming from the TV in the den.

Dad said, "Nah, I'm good."

"Leave the phone unplugged." Mom headed for the door.
"We'll be back in an hour."

We drove down to Joe's Ices—lemon for Mom,
strawberry-lime for me—and looked out at the bay. You could
see the city skyline—all twinkling and exciting and terrifying—
and a bunch of boats on their way to who knows where. I
thought about all the creatures beneath the water's surface
and wondered whether or not the fish and sharks down
there were doing any better than I was at slogging through life.

"I had this friend when I was about your age . . . ,"
Mom said, as we sat at a picnic table with our ices.

"Mom," I said. "Please don't."

She looked at me and I thought for sure she was just
going to tell her story anyway, but she just smiled and

ran a hand over my hair. "You know I love you, right?"

"Of course." I looked away.

When fireworks started to light the sky, we grabbed the quilt we kept in the car and moved to the little beach, watching as colors and shapes appeared and then burned out.

Mom drove us home with the windows down and the radio blaring a song about a place where the streets have no name. She sang along, her hands so tight on the wheel that I thought it must hurt. The song was still playing when I got out of the car in front of our house, but Mom showed no signs of turning off the engine. She stayed there in the driver's seat, perfectly still, until the last note. I waited for her on the porch.

When I couldn't sleep because of a phantom phone ringing in my ear, I got up and stood in my PJs in the middle of my room, playing Russia with an imaginary ball. I made it all the way through sixies—pretending to throw under my arm, pretending to catch in front, six times— before getting back into bed.

Now I prayed for the end of the world to be swift and to happen while I slept, so that I'd never have to leave the house again.

I dreamt that baby cicadas had nested in my hair and that Mom had to spend hours upon hours combing them out.

10.

Mom told me over breakfast that I had to apologize to Alyssa for throwing the ball at her. "You must be joking."

"Afraid not." She took her dish of toast crumbs to the trash and brushed them off.

"Even after the phone ringing torture of last night?" My cereal was already too soggy, inedible. Then when I saw the newspaper on the table—with a big headline that read SWARMS! and a picture of hundreds of huge flying bugs— I lost my appetite completely.

Those holes Peter had shown me. He'd said it was just a matter of days.

Mom turned and leaned against the counter. "Other people's bad behavior isn't an excuse for your own."

"But I'm not sorry," I said. Then she launched into a whole speech about how violence is never the answer, but I was stealing glimpses at those bugs and at the article, about millions of newly hatched insects just south of us.

"This is non-negotiable," she concluded. "I'll come with you if you want."

"And bring brownies?"

"Yeah," she said dryly. "As it turns out I'm not going to be doing that."

I dumped my cereal and knew this was a standoff I'd never win. "I'll go. Alone."

I got dressed and rang Alyssa's doorbell, and when she answered I knew 100 percent from the smug look on her face that she was the one who'd made the calls. She held an ice pack up to her face and I wanted to say, *Oh, gimme a break!*

An ice pack! A day later!

"Mom!" she called out.

I stiffened. I hadn't been expecting *that*. I heard footsteps behind her and quickly said, "I came to say I'm sorry."

Just so there was no confusion.

Her mom appeared. "This is her?"

I repeated, "I came to apologize."

"Well, isn't that big of you, Julie?" said Alyssa's mom.

I made myself smile. "Juli-*ah*."

Then I just waited for what was going to happen next

and started to wish that my mom *had* come with me.

"Go on, Lyss." The mom elbowed her.

Alyssa said, "Apology accepted."

"Great," her mom said. "And I assume nothing like this will happen again or I'll have to speak with your mother. Now why don't you two go play?"

Everything froze.

That's it? I wanted to scream.

She nudged Alyssa out the door. When Alyssa took away the ice pack and handed it to her mom, the bruise on her cheekbone made me feel *actually* sorry for a minute. Then Alyssa said, "You're just mad because we're better at Russia than you are."

My fingertips burned. *"What?"*

It was ridiculous. I wasn't interested in their game. That didn't mean they were better at it than me. "I could totally beat you at Russia."

She stood. "Is that a challenge?"

I shrugged like I owned it. "I guess it is."

"Well, come on." She went to a basket on the porch that had a few balls in it and grabbed two.

I said, "Not *now*."

"Why *not* now?"

"We need a referee or something. Someone to make sure neither of us takes any shortcuts."

She didn't look convinced, didn't want to give up her

obvious advantage. Her game. Her balls. Her turf. Her day and hour.

"It's only fair," I said.

"Okay." She thought for a minute. "Saturday afternoon. That's all the time you get."

"Fine. Whatever."

She said, "We'll ask Taylor."

"No way," I said. "Peter."

"Your boyfriend? Nu-uh. Andrew."

"Fine."

"What time?"

"I don't know. I'll text you."

"I don't have a phone."

"Of course you don't. Let's say noon." Then, for a second, Alyssa studied me with what look liked genuine curiosity. "What were you and Peter doing in the woods anyway?"

"Watching *End of Daze*." I felt bold—not only that I'd done it but that I was telling someone. "I'm not allowed at home so we've been sneaking off to watch, but you guys interrupted, so we've only seen the first episode."

"Fascinating." She crossed her arms.

"Did you watch episode two?" I felt my heart start to pump faster.

"Yeah."

"Who was on the other end of the phone? The mom's phone?"

"A man. He hung up. Mack thinks she must have been having an affair or something."

"Oh, jeez," I said.

Alyssa still had a ball in her hand and tossed it back into the basket. "I think Archer is going to die this week."

"No way. They wouldn't do that."

But Alyssa looked pretty confident.

"Do you think it could really happen?" I asked. "The end of the world?"

"Eventually, duh," Alyssa said, unconcerned. "I'm going in the pool."

I got up to leave and followed Alyssa's gaze over to Taylor's house, where I noticed the empty driveway. I remembered that Taylor had mentioned a doctor's appointment and got an idea: I could hang out with Alyssa all morning *without Taylor*. Maybe we'd gotten off on the wrong foot. Maybe without Taylor there we'd find some common ground. I was fascinating! She'd said so!

I said, all casual-like, "You want company?"

Alyssa stood there with a blank look on her face, and after what felt like a really, really, really long time, she said, "I guess."

"Okay." I worked hard not to look too excited. This was a totally awesome turn of events. "I'll be right back."

I bolted across the street to change into my suit.

"Where's the fire?" Mom said from her seat at the kitchen table.

"We're going swimming."

"Who's we?"

"Me and Alyssa."

Mom sipped her coffee, typed a few things on her laptop. "She apologized? For the funny business with the phone?"

I nodded but not really. "Everything's fine again."

"I'm not sure it was ever fine to begin with," she said. "But I'm proud of you for apologizing."

"We can't even be sure it was her," I said. "It could have been anyone."

She gave me that look. The look that always went right through me, like when I was caught in a lie or trying to make an excuse not to do something around the house that I really knew I should do. "What?" I said.

"You really don't want me to answer that question." She clicked around, typed some more.

"Can I go?"

"I guess so." She typed some more. "But I want you home for lunch."

I checked the clock. Time was going too fast and Taylor would probably be home soon. "Mom, that's like an hour and a half from now."

"Indeed, it is."

There was no point in arguing. I'd only be wasting time.

I changed into my suit and ran back across the street

and rang Alyssa's bell, but nobody answered. I heard a shriek from out back so I walked around the house and to the pool.

"Look who's back," the mom said. Her skin was shiny in the sun and her bleached hair looked almost yellow. She was sitting in a lounge chair holding a metallic sheet that was aiming more of the sun's rays at her face. The grass seed on the lawn hadn't really taken and the whole place looked thirsty.

Alyssa was in the pool and climbed up onto an inflatable tube and splashed me. It was cold, but I jumped right in.

Alyssa was laughing when I surfaced. "You seriously still hold your nose?"

I hadn't even realized I had. "Not all the time." It sounded so lame, and then we had nothing else to say, and I wondered why she let me come over if she was going to keep on being mean to me.

With her floating around in the tube, it was hard to know what I was supposed to do, so I just swam around. Her mother said, "Well, this is all too exciting for my blood," and disappeared inside.

After a little more swimming I said, "Want to play Russia? Only for, you know, practice."

"I guess." Alyssa paddled over to the steps and got out of the tube and pool without getting herself wet again.

We were both up to sevensies—I was starting to hate all that bouncing—when Alyssa said, "Do you wear a bra?"

I froze. "No."

She studied me. "I guess you don't really need one like I do." She threw her ball way high. "Taylor's mom is taking her shopping for one after the doctor's."

How had Taylor not told me about that? After we'd spent the entire last year waiting and hoping for our bodies to start changing?

The ball smacked back into Alyssa's hand.

We went up to her room after a while and she plopped down in her hot pink ALYSSA chair, leaving me nowhere to sit but her bed, which was Queen size and covered in a silky black-and-pink jungle-patterned spread with a deep pink border. Her huge stuffed giraffe was in a far corner and didn't seem babyish after all, but more like some designer's touch to perfect the cool safari theme. Her walls didn't have any posters or pictures, just a set of big letters—also pink—that spelled out her name.

"What should we do?" I asked, thinking, *She sure does like her name.*

"I don't know. Want to spy on my neighbors?"

"No!"

"It's nothing to get all scaredy-cat about."

"I just don't want to."

"All right, fine," she said. "What *do* you want to do? Play with *dolls* or something?"

So. Mean.

"Let's watch TV," I said, noticing the flat screen on the wall above her dresser.

"All right." She tossed me the remote like she was already too bored for words. "Knock yourself out." She flipped through a few pages of a magazine. "Beating you at Russia is going to be like taking candy from a baby."

More flipping.

Flip, like in slow motion.

"An *actual baby*."

How could I be so stupid? How had I read this all wrong?

"I'm not actually sorry I threw the ball at you." I stood up. "Not at all."

She looked up, her mouth hanging open.

Flip.

I managed, "My mom *made me* come over to apologize."

I knew I had to leave before I either got beat up or cried.

Her eyes returned to her magazine. "Then why are you still here?"

I tossed the remote onto her bed as I left the room. "Good question."

"I'll see you Saturday!" Alyssa called out after me, all fake cheery. "If you have the guts to even show up!"

11.

Mom had made tuna salad with celery and onion in it, and she was setting the table when I got home.

"Fancy," I said, because lunch didn't usually involve placemats. I wondered if I appeared nervous about what I'd just done.

She said, "Oh!" and put a third and fourth placemat down. "Wendy called for you, and I got her mom on the line and invited them over."

"Mo-om." This was the last thing I needed. What I needed was more Russia practice, and fast.

"What? It's fun to be spontaneous. And you haven't seen Wendy since school let out. Besides, they say the cicadas are coming tomorrow or—"

"I'm so sick of waiting for these cicadas." I slid into a kitchen chair.

"I would think you'd be a little bit more excited about something that only happens once every seventeen years. It's a scientific wonder!"

I rolled my eyes. This was all a good cover for how sick I felt.

She studied me and I thought she was going to say, "What happened?" or "Why do you look like you've seen a ghost?" But she just said, "Go run a comb through your hair or something. And change out of your suit for lunch."

Upstairs, I changed and brushed my hair and opened the drawer of my desk and put back that picture of me and Wendy. In it, we were sitting on lounge chairs in her backyard, holding fancy old-fashioned fans and wearing silly hats. That might have been the day I'd invented Millionaire. Maybe it would be good to see Wendy after all.

"Julia!" Mom called after the doorbell rang. I went out into the hall and down the stairs and into a hug from Wendy and then her mom.

"Come on." Mom grabbed the placemats off the kitchen table. "Let's have lunch out back instead."

We talked about the cicadas as we ate, and about the vacation Wendy's family was taking that fell right smack in the middle of music camp.

"We leave the day after it starts and get back the day before the concert," Wendy said.

"She's so disappointed," her mom said. "But what can you do?"

"Well, we'll bring Wendy to the concert if she wants?" Mom looked at Wendy. "We'll get an extra ticket and you can come see Julia and the rest of your friends from school?"

"That'd be fun," Wendy said. "Thanks, Mrs. Richards."

After lunch, the moms decided to go inside to talk about some curtain project my mom was cooking up. Wendy and I sat under the table umbrella in awkward silence for a minute. I wasn't sure whether it was all in my head— if it was just me being awkward because of Russia and Alyssa—or both of us. I was relieved Wendy wouldn't be at camp if we were this miserable around each other; hopefully she'd just forget about the concert by the time it rolled around. Finally I said, "You want to go swimming?"

"If you want." She shrugged a pale shoulder. Wendy was a girl who knew her way around a bottle of sunscreen.

I stopped myself from shrugging back. But it was true that I didn't really care one way or the other. I went swimming every day, and it wasn't even that hot out.

"I brought my clarinet," she said. "We could play some duets."

"Maybe later." I wasn't in the mood.

"I got new stickers." She reached for her beachy tote bag. "You won't believe how much the piña colada scratch-'n'-sniff ones actually smell like piña colada."

Scratch 'n' sniff! She was still into stickers.

"How do you know what a piña colada smells like?" I snapped.

"I just do," she said.

Why was I being so mean? What was wrong with stickers?

The wind rustled the leaves overhead and we were quiet again. Then Wendy said, "So what have you been doing? Did you do any of the summer reading yet?"

"No, mostly I hang out with Taylor and this new girl who moved in across the street. Alyssa. She knows this game you play with a ball. It's called Russia. I can show you if you want."

"Maybe later."

"I could use the practice," I said, and then I braved it. "I'm going head to head with her this weekend."

"Why?"

I could tell from the way she said it that she didn't care, and I didn't see the point of trying to explain everything that had been going on, even though Wendy would totally *understand* what it was like to be made fun of for freckles or holding your nose or a flat chest. I guess I didn't want Wendy to tell me how weird it all sounded and how I should just stop hanging out with them because they sounded horrible. Because even if that was true, this was where I lived, and Taylor was still my best friend. Not hanging out with them wasn't really an option.

"Maybe we *should* go swimming," Wendy said.

"Yeah. Let's."

For a while things seemed almost fun and I forgot about Alyssa. Wendy and I raced each other and tried to do cartwheels underwater, and I told her all about *The Haunted Pond* and she was totally into it. I told her, too, about how I now officially had a crush on Peter and how we had been sneaking his Dad's iPad out to watch *End of Daze*.

"Yikes," she said. "Really?"

"Yeah, it's awesome. Scary but awesome."

"I'm not allowed to watch it."

"I figured."

I watched my beach ball glide across the surface of the pool. Wendy was lying on a raft and the ball bumped into her, so she nudged it with an elbow and it came back my way. The sun was warmest on my thighs, and when the ball hit my elbow I popped it up in the air like I was a seal.

Upstairs, later, Wendy wailed, "Oh, no! What happened to your unicorn poster?"

"Oh. It fell and ripped."

"I *loved* that poster." She stood in the middle of my room, and I could see now that she was starting to develop even though I wasn't. It made me want to strangle her.

Wendy said, "And something else is different."

"Well, I'm probably moving to the other room soon."

"Oh, no! Really?" She looked suddenly concerned and seemed to be waiting for an explanation.

I was entirely confused. "Why 'oh no'? It's going to be awesome."

She looked like I'd said just the wrong thing, and looked away. "Oh, yeah, totally. Forget I said anything."

"Wendy." I waited for her to look at me. "What's going on?"

She sighed. "You can't tell anybody I told you."

"Okay. I won't."

She looked away again. "My mom thought your mom was going to have another baby. I guess she was wrong. You can't tell them I told you."

Everything got blurry. Then I thought about the weirdness about the room down the hall—the way it was so mysterious, so complicated. They had thought it was going to be a baby's room. And now . . . it wasn't? Because Dad had told me he was working on it, the room. So what did *that* mean?

Maybe that was something they still wanted? Another kid?

I liked the idea of it.

Someone to be lonely with.

"I'm sorry," Wendy said. "I think my mom thought there'd be official news today, that that was why we were invited."

"No," I said. "No news."

I didn't want to talk about it anymore. "Let's just play Spit, okay?"

"Your carousel!" Wendy practically screamed, noticing, I guessed, the circle of missing dust on my dresser when she got up to get the cards. "Did it break?"

"No. I still have it."

"Oh, good. I thought maybe there'd been an earthquake that only hit your room or something."

I said, "That would be pretty crazy," but as we started to play cards, I felt like I was experiencing some serious tremors and aftershocks. I could barely shuffle the deck.

"So." Wendy lowered her voice. "I finally got a bra."

"That's great. I'm happy for you." And then we just played and played while I struggled to hold it together.

"I broke my Dopey," I said, after a while. "You know, the Seven Dwarfs I've had since I was little?"

"Stinks." Wendy was going to town with fours and fives and sixes on one of the piles, but I had nothing to add, just jacks and queens and some nines and tens. "I bet your mom can fix it."

When Wendy and her mom were gone, I helped clean up more than I ever did without being told to.

"Well, aren't you helpful," Mom said. She never missed a beat.

I wanted to ask her about the office, the baby's room, whether that was happening or not and if not, what had happened. I wanted to tell her that I'd dug my own grave over at Alyssa's. But I couldn't get the courage up.

I *did* find myself just brave enough to say, "I was wondering if we could go shopping."

"What for?" She was washing plastic tumblers in the sink.

I lowered my voice. "A bra."

"Oh, honey." She turned to me. "When you need one, we'll go."

She'd used that line a few times when I'd asked about a cell phone, too, but I didn't remind her of that, or of how ridiculous an argument it was. I wanted to stay focused.

"Mom." My ears felt like they were on fire. "I'm telling you I need one."

She looked up—almost like she didn't recognize me at all—and then her features softened. "Okay, then. Tomorrow morning?"

12.

I was up and dressed and ready to hit the mall in record time Thursday morning. But when we got to the store and Mom asked a saleswoman to show us to the "training bras," I wanted to curl up and die. Or, at the very least, tell Mom to forget the whole thing and just go for a cinnamon bun instead. The wide grin of the saleswoman—a grandmother type—didn't help.

"Mom," I said, when she tried to follow me into the fitting room. "I think I can handle it from here."

I ended up having a hard time with the clasps, so the whole thing was taking a while.

"Julia." Mom's voice was so close. "I can help."

"I can do it!" Could this be any more awkward? I thought I might dislocate my shoulder. Then it finally hooked.

The first one was too tight around my back, though, and the second one, too big in the cup. I handed them over the door and held my hands over my chest as if she could see through the door. "I need something in between these."

"I'll be right back." A minute later Mom handed another bra over the top. It fit just right.

"This is the one," I said when I came out, dressed again and feeling strangely naked under my top.

"Okay." She was all business. "We'll get a few more in this same size."

Normally, I tried to stay at the mall as long as possible if it meant the possibility of Mom buying things for me, even if it really was just a cinnamon bun. But today I just wanted to get home so I could go to my room, put one of my bras on, and study myself in the mirror. Maybe it was true that I didn't really need one, but maybe having one would trick my body into changing that.

I was lying on a float in the pool later in the day, feeling dozy after swimming a bunch of laps, when the phone rang. I braced myself for a hang-up, for it all to start again. But instead Mom called out, "Julia? It's Peter. He says his mom made cookies and do you want to go over for a while?"

That pepped me right up. "Sure!"

I hurried upstairs to change and headed out to Peter's, my hair still damp.

He was sitting on the front porch with the iPad resting on his bony knees. "Hope you didn't have your heart set on cookies."

I smiled. "Cookies are overrated."

He got up. "Let's go."

He hopped onto his skateboard, and I walked beside him. "Hey, can you teach me to do that—skateboard—sometime?"

"Sure. Whenever you want."

So we found our spot by the pond and we sat and watched episode two.

Alyssa had told me the truth, at least. After Mack picked up his dead wife's phone and there was a man on the other end who said, "Sorry, wrong number," and hung up, Mack started to suspect an affair. He and Archer went back to their apartment, in a building now surrounded by bodies and uncollected trash, and Mack went through his wife's things, looking for more proof. Archer was only about six years old, so he went to his room and started to play with Legos, and I got to thinking how nice it would be, to be young enough that when the world was ending, you could still find a way to play with Legos and not just sit around freaking out.

After that, though, I started to have a hard time concentrating. There was a new story line that followed some other survivors in another city. A couple of the guys looked the same, and I was having trouble remembering which one was which.

"I'm going head to head against Alyssa in Russia on Saturday," I said when the show was over and Peter closed the iPad cover.

"What? Because you threw the ball at her?"

"I don't even know." I stood up to stretch and told him about my mom forcing me to apologize and then me taking it back. "Alyssa said I was mad that I wasn't good at Russia, so I told her I could beat her."

"Julia, Julia, Julia." Peter shook his head.

"What?"

He just shook his head some more.

"It's complicated," I said. I started to think that maybe that was something people just said when they really didn't want to explain anything for real. Because, sure, Peter knew she'd been "mean" to me, but I didn't want to tell him all the gory details, like about the prank calls or the fact that Alyssa had made fun of my freckles and flat chest and clothes and bedroom and the fact that I held my nose that *one time*—or that she hadn't exactly come out and said it, but how I knew she thought I was ugly and that no boys would ever like me.

A strong, warm wind blew and the leaves overhead sounded like their own kind of swarm. I looked up and wondered whether bugs were going to start raining from the sky, and shivered at the thought of it, but they didn't.

"I guess you'll need a coach," Peter said, and I smiled.

We went to his backyard patio and ran through the whole game so that he knew all the moves. He picked out nines for me to focus on, and I did it maybe thirty times without dropping the ball once.

"Good work," he said when it was time for me to head home.

Maybe it was a weird, random thing to be proud of, but I felt that way anyway.

13.

I sprang out of bed on Friday and started practicing
Russia in the backyard. I didn't think about Taylor or
Alyssa or the prank calls or candy or babies or anything.
None of it mattered but the game. Nothing mattered
but concentrating on throwing the ball just so, and
staying focused.

Tomorrow, if I could pull this off, everything would
be different.

When I was completing my seventh turn-clap-turn
move, ready to go for the first time onto eightsies, Peter said
"Hey!" and I dropped the ball.

"Crap." I chased after it. "You made me miss!"

"Sorry," he said. "I'm coming over." He pushed something
up to the fence and climbed onto a tree that bordered

our yards—the trunk was on his side—and dropped down on my side like a bag of limbs in an orange T-shirt. "That used to be easier."

"You could have walked around."

"Takes too long." He fixed his shirt. "How's it going?"

"Feeling good. I think."

He ran a hand through his hair, brushing out a leaf, and I wondered if boys' hair felt different than girls' and how long it would be before I found out. He said, "Let's see what you've got," and sat in one of our loungers and pulled up his sweat socks.

I started the whole game over.

I got up to tens without dropping anything.

Peter said, "She's just jealous, you know."

I snorted. "Of *what*?"

Boys could be so dumb.

"Of you, you idiot."

It was hard to count my Russia moves while talking so I stopped midway through tens. "Why would anyone be jealous of *me*?"

He blushed a little, I swear he did, and said, "Because you're smart and, you know . . . pretty and stuff."

"She *doesn't* think I'm pretty." The very idea of it was ridiculous.

But then I thought: *He does.*

He does!

He *does*?

My mom brought us sandwiches around lunchtime and asked, "What's with all the balls lately?"

I always thought of my parents as sharing everything with each other, and the fact that Dad hadn't told Mom anything about our chat in the yard the other night surprised me some.

"Just a game," I said. "It's called Russia."

I explained the basics, leaving out the bit about the showdown and Peter being my coach.

"Wait, wait, wait," she said. "I know this! I used to play it. Or something like it! But we called it something different." She pinched her head with her fingers. "Oh, what was it. Onesies, twosies. No! Leansies Clapsies, Onesies Twosies. Wow. That takes me back. That was a *long time* ago."

It was a little embarrassing how excited she was.

"Well, that's good," she said on her way back inside. "It's better than reading trashy magazines, at any rate."

I felt bad not telling her the whole story, about Alyssa and me being on a path to mutual destruction, but I was too busy feeling hopeful to do anything about it. Because if Mom had been any good at Leansies Clapsies—talk about a ridiculous name—maybe Russia was in my blood.

My arms were jellyfish, but I only had a day to get ready, so I got right back to work.

I was about to throw my last thirteen out of thirteen in what would be my first ever successful run through the entire game when Peter said, "Julia?"

From the way he said it, I thought he was going to say something like, "Don't move. There's a massive cicada on your back," so I froze.

"Are you wearing a bra?" He was smiling.

"Oh, jeez," I moaned and looked away. "Shut up!"

"Sor-ry," he said. "You look nice is all."

I was no doubt redder than a tomato for real. "I said to shut up!"

"All right, already. Jeez yourself." Then after a minute, he said, "Do you hear that?"

There was a buzzing sound in the air, faint but distinct, like an electric generator whirring.

"What is it?" I asked.

"The cicadas are really hatching."

"I'm not impressed."

I threw my last thirteen and caught it.

Peter cheered.

After I helped Dad cover the pool out back after dinner—I bet him ten dollars we'd be uncovering it in the morning—I went out front and saw Taylor on her lawn

with a box of sparklers. I walked over because I wanted her
to see that I had a bra now, too.

"Alyssa told me you went bra shopping." I could hear
in my own voice that I sounded sad, that I hated even saying
her name. I wanted to go back to last summer, when
Taylor and I wrote our names in the air with sparklers, and
tasted honeysuckle on our tongues, and didn't even
know that Alyssa existed.

"Yeah, so?" I could see the straps of a light pink
bra peeking out from under her tank top. I was sure the
straps were showing on purpose because I'd done the
same thing.

"So why didn't you tell me?" I asked.

"Didn't I?" She started writing something in the air with
her sparkler's glow.

"No. You didn't."

She looked at me differently and her gaze fell upon
my shoulders.

I stood up taller.

"You're such a copycat." She wrote something else in the
air with her sparkler.

"Yeah." I took a sparkler out of the box on the porch.
"And you're so original."

Her ghostly letters were barely there when I stepped to
her side and lit my sparkler off hers. "What'd you write?"

"Nothing."

I took my own sparkler and wrote the word PETER.
Then I wrote over it in midair with another word: PRETTY.
I watched the letters disappear into the buzzing night
air as little sparks flew off the wand, burning my hand just
a touch.

"So you probably heard about the Russia game tomorrow?"
My sparkler went dead. "Between me and Alyssa."

"Yeah, she told me."

"Are you going to come watch?"

"I don't know." She wasn't making eye contact.

"Oh, like you have other plans?"

"I said I don't know, Julia." She did a clicking thing
with her mouth. "You're never going to beat her. So why are
you even doing it?"

I puffed my chest out. "I might beat her!"

She raised her eyebrows. "I doubt it."

"Thanks for the support." I looked away.

"It's almost time for *End of Daze*." She picked up the box
of sparklers and said, "I guess I'll see you around."

"I'm watching it, too, you know. With Peter."

"Good for you, Julia." She went inside.

At home, my parents were settling in by the TV, so I said
good night and went up to bed. I wouldn't have wanted
to distract myself from tomorrow's mission with apocalyptic
images anyway.

All I cared about was tomorrow.

Throwing.

Catching.

Clapping.

Turning.

Touching.

Winning.

14.

I woke up excited, with a buzzing in my head. I went downstairs to eat a good breakfast for fuel and found my parents watching TV in their robes. On-screen, a local news anchor was being bombarded by big black bugs in front of the courthouse in town.

The buzzing wasn't only in my head.

"You, dear daughter, owe me ten bucks." Dad opened the blinds on the door to the deck; bug after bug banged into the screen.

I jumped back for a minute with a shriek, then recovered and moved closer again, to study them. They were huge, bigger than any bug I'd ever seen, and they seemed, well, pathetic. They just kept flying into the screen and falling away and then flying away or banging into it again. I slid the glass door open an inch, knowing the screen would protect us, and the sound was like a UFO hovering overhead.

So.

Very.

Loud.

It was really happening.

The pool cover was black with bugs, the air thick with them.

When I went to the couch, I sat close to Mom, tucking my feet under her thigh.

We all watched the footage again and listened to the anchorman bring new viewers up to speed, talking about how many millions of bugs had hatched overnight in however many square miles. He looked like he liked bugs about as much as I did.

"Looks like we're stuck inside today," Mom said.

Dad plopped down on the sofa. "I am so glad I don't have to attempt to get to work in this."

"But—"

The Russia showdown! I had worked so hard! I was ready!

But I looked outside again.

You could not play Russia with the air full of bugs. Was this an act of God? To save me the humiliation of this showdown?

My parents seemed unable to move from the news, and I decided to stay close. When the phone rang a while later, it was Mom who answered it on her way back from the bathroom.

I knew it was Alyssa. I knew it was time. But had she seen the news? Had she looked out her window?

Mom simply said, "That was Alyssa calling to cancel."

"Oh," I said. "Okay."

"What are you canceling?" she asked.

"Oh, just a game of Russia."

Canceled.

I wasn't sure whether I was relieved or not.

Did that mean it'd never happen or that we'd reschedule?

Either way it was out of my hands.

We stayed glued to the TV into the afternoon, watching the reporter ask random people for reactions to the bugs. Their answers were pretty boring after the first few. How many different ways could people be expected to say, "Wow. That's a lot of bugs"? There was one report of a car accident that the driver blamed on not being able to see because of bugs—"Ha!" Dad said, "Told you!"—but nobody had gotten hurt, and that was about as exciting as it got. So we kept the TV on low and starting playing board games—Life and Monopoly. It felt like a crazy snow day in the middle of summer, and I liked it.

When dinnertime came around and some of the stations put on their quiz shows and sitcoms, things started to feel normal again. So normal that I was about to ask if I could go over to Taylor's or something, but then I noticed the buzz again. It had been there all day, but I had gotten good at ignoring it. I looked out the sliding doors at the deck—they were still everywhere.

There was no way we were going anywhere.

Today, only the cicadas had won.

Later that night, too late, the doorbell rang. Mom pulled her robe on—she was already in her PJs—and shuffled to the door in her slippers. I peeked from the kitchen, where we'd been looking at a catalog of fall clothes, and saw Alyssa and her mother standing on the front porch, swatting bugs.

"I'm so sorry to bother you." Alyssa's mother's words sounded funny, loose.

"Oh, hi." Mom turned the porch light on but showed no signs of opening the screen door. "I've been meaning to come by to introduce myself and give you a proper welcome, but I've had this awful stomach thing."

My mother was a pro.

"Oh," Alyssa's mother said. "No worries. But, well, Alyssa's father's out of town until tomorrow, and I know the girls are friendly. Could she stay here for, I don't know"—she looked over her shoulder toward her house—"for an hour or two. I asked over at Taylor's, but it's just her and her father home tonight, so, you know. . . ."

"Oh." Mom still hadn't moved to open the door. "Is everything okay?"

"Sure, sure. It's just that something came up. So can you take her?" Alyssa and her mom were still swatting. The looks on their faces showed they didn't think it was as funny as I did.

"Of course," Mom said stiffly, and she tapped the screen a few times so that bugs jumped off. She opened the door, and Alyssa slipped in. Alyssa's mother was already gone, running back across the street with her hoodie pulled up over her head. She didn't even say good-bye.

Alyssa came in and sat at the kitchen table. She was wearing her pajamas under a light hoodie, and something about that made me sad for her. When it was clear she wasn't going to say anything, I finally said, "What's going on?"

"Nothing." She sighed. "What's going on with you?"

"Nothing."

I sat there, listening to the kitchen wall clock tick, trying to imagine where Alyssa's mother had to go so urgently. Coming up blank, I said, "You want some ice cream?"

"Sure."

"You want to watch a movie?"

"Sure."

So we fixed some bowls and started a movie. A few

minutes later, we were both laughing at the same joke. So maybe a truce was occurring; maybe we were powerless to stop it.

But then, during a boring part, Alyssa turned to me. "You know how you said you didn't think they were going to kill Archer?" She spoke louder. "You know, *End of Daze*?"

I shushed her; Mom was in the next room.

"Did you have nightmares like you thought you would?" She faked actual interest. "The mushroom cloud?"

Mom came in with some water for us, and I held my breath, praying for Alyssa to be quiet. "Oh, thank you, Mrs. Richards," she said, and she seemed to smile at herself when my mom was gone again.

So she didn't actually want to rat me out; she just wanted me to know that she could. How could I have been so foolish as to trust her with my secret?

Luckily, she just watched the movie quietly. All the while my stomach felt like a mushroom cloud, exploding in on itself.

When the doorbell rang two hours later—we were all so very tired—Alyssa's last words to me were, "Don't think you're off the hook. We'll reschedule when the bugs are gone. I don't want to be dealing with all their dead bodies. So gross."

She took off like the house was on fire, and Mom turned to Alyssa's mom and said, "Actually, there was something

I wanted to talk to you about."

Mom stepped out onto the front porch and closed the real door behind her.

Whatever they were talking about, it couldn't be good. Because I'd ratted Alyssa out, hadn't I? About the money and the naked neighbors. And if my mom so much as mentioned any of that, let alone accused Alyssa of making prank calls, I'd be destroyed for sure.

I couldn't sleep despite exhaustion—couldn't block out the buzzing, couldn't get Russia out of my head.

I tried counting sheep.

I tried counting cicadas as they bounced off the window above my bed.

I tried fantasizing about a postnuclear holocaust romance with Peter.

I tried reading the book I didn't want to end.

But nothing could stop my brain from picturing the ball, flying away and then back to me.

It felt like some kind of madness, some disease.

Russia wouldn't let me go.

I wasn't off the hook.

Not yet.

15.

By 11:00 a.m. on Sunday—Mom had refused to attempt to get to church—Dad was officially stir-crazy. He'd spent the morning pacing in front of the doors to the backyard, checking on bug activity, and then finally decided that they seemed to be calming down. So he announced that we were going to the mall for lunch. "It'll be great," he said. "I need socks."

My dad always seemed to need socks.

We all got ready and grabbed hoodies, even though it was eighty-five degrees out. We went to the garage through the door off the hall near the kitchen and got into the car, which we hardly ever brought in there, but with the bugs coming, Dad had planned ahead. As the garage door opened, the sun came in and I think some bugs flew in, too. We pulled out and it sounded like a downpour. There were still more bugs out than I'd thought, which meant no Russia would be played today. Alyssa's driveway was empty anyway.

Once we were on the road, Dad tried the wipers a few times, but they were useless. When we came to stops at red lights or signs, I swore I heard crunching under the wheels. When we picked up some speed on the highway, there seemed to be less bugs. But there were still a handful of them, dinging off cars and trucks and then spiraling to the ground like tiny doomed fighter pilots. I cracked my window and the noise outside was so very loud, like there was a beehive in my ears.

Eventually Dad pulled into the mall parking lot up close to the main entrance. "Why don't you two get out?"

Mom and I both pulled on our hoodies and ran for the door and had to swat some bugs away—I screamed—and then we made it through the big glass doors into the entryway and started laughing.

"This is pretty crazy," I said.

"See! I told you!" She elbowed me and her look turned all dreamy. "I remember it now, from when I was younger, not like seventeen years ago, but the one before that, when I was like eight. I'd forgotten or maybe blocked it out. I remember being at my grandmother's house and not going outside for days, but it was almost like she didn't even let me know why we weren't going out. I remember the noise, though. We spent days doing this art project, building this whole little fairy village. I should really be more crafty. We should. Together."

"Okay, Mom. We'll be sure to do that."

She fixed a piece of my hair, pushing it off my shoulder. "Don't be like that."

I thought about asking her what she had talked to Alyssa's mom about, but thought I might be better off not knowing.

Dad ran to us through the parking lot, and then we were all three in the mall, walking along a shiny white floor that reflected overhead fluorescent lights and the colored lights of store signs. Everyone and their uncle was there, and I felt sick thinking it was possible—likely, even—that Alyssa would be here. Her car was gone and her mom loved the mall. But it was a big place. With any luck, we wouldn't see them.

So we bought some socks for my dad and we got a few new T-shirts for camp/school, and we bumped into a family we knew from church and a girl I knew from school, then Mom lingered too long at the window display at some baby store. Of course they'd want a baby to be closer to their bedroom. But obviously that wasn't happening. If it were, there would have been signs. Like Mom would have gained weight or lost weight. She'd have cut out the half a beer with dinner. I didn't know if or how heartbroken they were or weren't, though, so I didn't really know how to feel except that I felt bad for bugging her about moving into the room so much.

We ended up in one of those annoying restaurants where the waiters all gather around and make a fuss for people's birthdays, but they can't sing "Happy Birthday" for some nutty legal reason, and so they clap out this rhythm and shout instead. It happened maybe three times before we'd even gotten our food, and again when we were finishing up. There was a lot of loud whooping this time around, and I craned my neck to see what the fuss was about.

Almost magically, I made eye contact with Taylor. Who was next to Alyssa. Who was next to her mom, who had an ice cream sundae with a candle stuck into it in front of her. She blew it out and shouted, "It's great to be thirty," and some people laughed. She kissed the man next to her, and I got my first glimpse of Alyssa's father. His hair was buzz-cut short and his arms were seriously at least twice the size of my dad's. I had a quick vision of them having a fistfight, and of my dad losing.

I slid farther into the booth so Alyssa wouldn't be able to see me. I suddenly very much didn't want to reschedule our game. I asked the waiter for the check myself.

"Where's the fire?" Dad said.

"No fire," I said, but I felt like there were flames under my feet.

We managed to escape without actually bumping into them, and I kept saying in my head, *I wouldn't want to go to Alyssa's mom's party anyway.* I put it on a loop to the same rhythm of the birthday clapping in the restaurant the whole ride home, even as the bugs hit the windshield, even as I felt like my stomach was a double-knotted shoelace.

Dad didn't want to open the garage door and let more bugs in so he said we were just going to make a run for it. He went first, keys in hand, and Mom ran after him. I didn't feel like running the thirty feet from the car to the door, though. So I put my hoodie on again and put the hood up and just walked at a regular pace—maybe even slower than normal.

There were bugs on the ground along the path, and I walked on tippy-toes to avoid them—each one easily bigger than my thumb. I felt bad for them, flapping around there, looking for mates without a clue as to what was really going on around them, oblivious to the fact that everybody hated them and that as soon as they mated and laid eggs, they would die.

I felt one bing me on the head and I wondered if maybe they knew more than I could imagine.

I stopped and shook myself off on the front porch while Mom said, "Hurry, hurry, hurry," from behind the screen door.

I thought about pulling the wings off one of the bugs

on the porch, to see what would happen to its head, but then Mom opened the door and the moment passed.

A while later, I heard noise on the street and went to the window, standing back so no one could see. Alyssa's car was back, and I watched as Taylor got out and ran down the block toward home, swatting bugs the whole way. I don't even know why, but I laughed.

16.

My mom and Peter's mom had formed a carpool for camp. Every morning of that first week, it was my mom's job to get us to the school where camp was and then Peter's mom's job to get us home. Week two would be the reverse. When Peter crunched his way up to the front porch Monday morning and rang the bell, I was ready.

"Did you do that thing?" I asked. "With the wings."

"Nah." He kicked a bug off the porch. "It seemed like a weird thing to do. But it's definitely true that it works."

"How can you be sure?"

"The Internet, Julia. Ever hear of it?" He grinned.

I pinched his arm.

He turned and looked at the lawn, still dotted with bugs. "To be honest, the whole thing is a little bit of a letdown."

"You think?" *Poor Peter*, I thought. No zombies and now more disappointment. "I actually find it more impressive than I thought I would."

"Why?"

"I don't know." I took a minute to think about it. "I guess I didn't realize I'd have *feelings* about them. Like I had dreams about them, and I feel bad for them but also think they're pathetic. I've never really thought so much about bugs before, and what a sad thing it is that they're just programmed to do what they do."

"We're all just programmed."

"Maybe"—I was pretty good in biology at school and knew about genes and DNA—"but I like to think I can at least shake things up every once in a while, you know. Do something unexpected."

"Yeah, like what?"

I knew it was wrong, but I smiled anyway. "Like throw a ball at somebody's face."

Peter laughed. "Yeah, that was pretty unexpected. I assume it got canceled?"

I nodded. "She wants to reschedule when the bugs and carcasses are all gone."

"That should give you at least another week to practice." Peter nodded. "So that's good, right?"

"I guess." But I really just wanted it to be over with.

My mom came out and said, "Well, good morning, Peter."

He said, "Good morning, Mrs. Richards," and we got into the car. They chitchatted most of the way, and we all talked about the cicadas. For once, now that it was actually happening and would soon be over, I didn't mind.

Camp was being held at the high school that we would all go to, so I took special note of things, like the colors of the lockers (finger-paint blue) and the smell (Lysol/fresh paint). I tried to imagine myself—older and wiser— walking in there for the first time even though it wouldn't *technically* be the first time. I hoped I'd be a totally different person by then and that maybe *this* place would be the place where I'd feel like I belonged. If there were any clues as to whether that would be the case, I couldn't see them.

Peter and I signed in and parted ways as we said hi to some people we knew from band at school. I looked around for Wendy before I remembered she wouldn't be there, and saw mostly unfamiliar faces since the camp drew from schools all around the island. Among those faces, one was smiling and bright. It belonged to a girl that had a short black bob haircut, short-short bangs, and a short denim skirt. She was wearing a cool graphic T-shirt with skyscrapers all over it, and was talking to a few girls who were laughing at whatever she was saying.

When one of the directors told us to break down into instrument groups and gave room assignments, I headed for the clarinet room and took a seat with some others. The overhead lights hummed ever so slightly while we waited quietly for instruction.

So quietly.

Too quietly.

Everybody was first-day awkward.

Then skyscraper girl came in and sat down next to me, and I got crazy nervous.

She got up and smoothed the back of her skirt, and sat again. Then she did the whole thing one more time. Everyone was staring at her, and when she noticed that, she looked at me and said, "It's a good thing all the flutes are ladies, otherwise some flute boys would be getting quite a show later today."

I laughed. "Wearing a skirt probably not the smartest move."

She laughed back and that was that.

Her name was Laney, and we grabbed time to talk between pull-out groups and individual assessments and had lunch together. We made a list of boys that we thought were cute even though we didn't know most of their names so we had to write things like "Broody Basoonist" and "Little Drummer Boy." She agreed that Peter was cute, and that I had what she called "crush dibs," and we confessed that we'd both just gotten our first bras and had never been kissed. We talked about the cicadas and about *End of Daze*, which she hadn't been allowed to watch, so I filled her in, and then it turned out she'd read the book about the haunted pond, too. We were like sisters who'd just never met, which, of course, we hadn't because we lived about as far from each other as you could while still living on the same island.

So unfair! She wasn't even zoned for this high school!

At the end of the day, while we were waiting for our rides—her older brother was hers and I thought that just made her even cooler—I told her about Alyssa and how her moving to my block had wrecked everything with Taylor and just in general, too. I told her about the stuffed giraffe and the ALYSSA chair, and the hairy guy and the woman who needed the boob job.

Laney's eyes got huge. "She *spies* on them?"

I nodded. I wasn't sure whether she was grossed out or impressed.

"Yuck," she said with a shake of her head.

Lastly, I told her about the Russia showdown. How I'd gotten myself into this totally weird situation where I was supposed to prove my worth by playing a weird ball game against a girl I despised.

"That's pretty messed up," Laney said.

"Should I back out?" I did not tell her I'd thrown a ball into Alyssa's face because I did not want to appear to be the psycho that maybe I was. "Or maybe she'll just forget about it?"

"Not likely." She shook her head violently. "And no way. You'll never live it down if you back out. Have you been practicing?"

I nodded. "A ton. Before the bugs anyway."

Peter joined us where we were sitting on a curb in the parking lot. "I've been coaching her," he said.

"Is she any good?" Laney asked him.

"She totally is," Peter said.

Laney nodded. "Well, then, you *have* to beat her."

I knew it to be true.

The week took on a steady rhythm, like time was a metronome, and I started to hear songs and notes and drum beats in my head instead of bouncing balls hitting concrete and palm flesh. I'd forgotten that I *loved* playing with a concert band. I liked the way I knew exactly what to do and started to wish the world were more like an orchestra, everybody knowing their role.

"I wish I could move to your block," Laney said on the last day of the first week, when we were waiting outside with Peter again. "Wouldn't that be awesome? Or even your neighborhood, so we'd go to high school together at least."

She and Peter were making me do the tensies move from Russia like a million times—bouncing and slapping,

TARA ALTEBRANDO

bouncing and slapping—against a wall near the parking lot.
There were bug carcasses on the school grounds, but
not a ton.

I said, "That would be amazing."

But it was a crazy fantasy. In reality, I felt dread of the
weekend creeping in. I hadn't really seen either Taylor or Alyssa
all week, and I'd gotten used to it. More than that, I'd liked it.

"You think it'll happen this weekend?" Laney asked.
She and Peter were as eager for news of the rescheduled
game as I was.

"It's possible."

I dropped my ball and Peter fetched it and bounced it
back to me.

Laney said, "Well, just remember that clarinet players
totally rule the world."

"Trumpets are pretty great, too," Peter said.

"Band geeks for the win!" I said and we all laughed.

When our rides came, we said see ya. And the second
Peter's mom pulled out onto the street, I missed Laney
so much it hurt.

My mom had a teeth cleaning scheduled that afternoon, so the plan was for me to go to Peter's until she
got home. He had prepared by downloading last Friday's

episode—we were a full week behind—but it started to drizzle on the ride home so the woods were not an option. Instead, we went downstairs, turned on the Wii, and turned the volume up loud. We took turns bowling so that the Wii kept making noises, but our attention was really on *End of Daze*. Peter's mom was too busy getting dinner ready upstairs to notice.

In this episode, Mack and Archer and the guys I couldn't tell apart in the other story line ended up meeting on a deserted highway. And the leader of the other group didn't seem to like Mack's attitude much. So there was a lot of tension and a lot of intense stares and glares. As much as I agreed that Mack had a lot of attitude, I figured you needed some of that if you were going to survive a nuclear-chemical apocalypse. In the end, Mack had to play nice with the guys because they had medical supplies and Archer had gotten a pretty big gash while playing on some old, rusty abandoned car. Or at least they thought it was abandoned . . . but then there was some thumping coming from the truck and they all gathered around— some of the guys had guns—to open it.

Roll credits.

"That's *it*?" I shouted.

"A cliffhanger!" Peter announced. "Surprise! Surprise!"

I fell back onto the couch cushions. "Ugh! This show drives me crazy."

"Well, it's on tonight. So we shouldn't have to wait long."

"This weekend?"

"Sure. I'll be in touch."

Then we bowled a bit for real.

When I got home, Mom said that Alyssa had called.

I stopped in my tracks. "What did she want?"

"She wanted to play that game with you, I guess, tomorrow." Mom was setting the table. Every night setting the table. "But we're having company so I told her no."

"What company?" My parents never told me anything.

"Aunt Colleen, and Mike and the kids. Melissa and George and the kids."

"*Mom,*" I moaned.

"What? It'll be fun." She took a plate of pork chops from the fridge. "So *anyway,* Alyssa suggested Sunday morning, but we have Mass. And then she said she had other plans Sunday, and after that, I guess she and her mother are going along on one of her father's trips for a few days."

I sat down on a kitchen chair. "Did she seem mad?"

"No," Mom said suspiciously. "Why would she be *mad*?"

"Oh, no reason."

Mom grabbed a beer from the fridge and opened the door to the deck. "I'm throwing these on the grill. Want to come out and keep me company?"

It was the last thing I wanted to do, really, but I did it anyway.

17.

Dad and I spent the morning getting the yard ready, which meant uncovering the pool and getting rid of bug carcasses. I thought they were crazy not to just reschedule since there was so much clean-up to do and some stray bugs still out there looking for love. But these were friends they only saw a few times a year, and I guess the planets had to be aligned for everybody to get together. None of the kids was even remotely my age.

Mom really went all out with the food, making all sorts of neat combinations of skewers, like beef and mandarin oranges, and chicken and limes. She made fresh lemonade and some other pink drink that was only for grown-ups.

I spent the first hour of the party playing tetherball with some of the boys, who were like eight or nine, then went swimming with five-year-old Isabel, the only girl. After that, she asked to see my room so we dried off and went upstairs.

I got out my carousel and turned on the music and lights for her, and her face lit up when she said, "It's *beautiful*."

After that I showed her my ballerina jewelry box, which I'd forgotten was a music box. We wound it up and listened as we watched the tiny pop-up ballerina inside twirl. The song playing was the same piece from *Swan Lake* I'd played that one afternoon, before the calls had started.

"I can do ballet." Isabel stood and put her arms up, fingertips touching to form an arch, and spun for me.

"Good job." I clapped and she just kept on twirling.

When she stopped, we both tried on some necklaces. Finally, I got out my Snow White and Dwarfs and she asked why there were only six. I went back to the drawer and showed her the many pieces of Dopey, and she looked like she was going to cry.

I said, "Don't worry. My mom's gonna help me fix it."

"I love your room," she said after a while, and I felt like an ungrateful person.

After playing with old Barbies, we went downstairs and sat next to each other in folding lawn chairs while eating ice cream sandwiches, and I taught Isabel how to play Millionaire. She was too young to be any good at it, but it was fun anyway, like when she said, "I have so much money you wouldn't even believe it. I have eighty twenty thousand and twenty hundred ten dollars."

The adults were right behind us, and Aunt Colleen was telling some old story about a birthday party she'd invited my mom to that my mom didn't go to.

"Not this again!" Mom said.

"*You* didn't think I was cool enough." Aunt Colleen sounded happy. "And you went to *Celia McGovern's* party instead."

"It wasn't *that*!" Mom was laughing.

"Oh, just admit it for once, will you?" Aunt Colleen said. "Now that we're old and gray."

They all laughed.

After everyone was gone, my parents sat outside for a while, just the two of them, while I went up to bed. I could hear their voices through the open bathroom window while I brushed my teeth. They were laughing a lot, and they sounded like something other than a husband and wife, something other than a mom and dad: they sounded like best friends.

Mom came up to my room a while later and sat on the edge of my bed. "You were really great with Isabel today. Thanks."

"She's cute," I said. I was really tired.

"So." Mom adjusted my bedspread. "I was thinking we'd spend some time in the office tomorrow, start cleaning it out, so you could move in there."

I woke right up.

This was *big*.

Huge!

I could see it all happening because I'd pictured it so many times before.

I knew where everything would go, what it would feel like to sleep in there for the first time. But the whole thing now made me sad. Because of what I knew.

"You're sure?" I said.

"Your father convinced me," she said. "And I know you're having a rough summer. This gives us a project!"

"Thank you thank you thank you," I said, and I sat up and gave her a huge, tight hug.

I changed into old clothes after Mass, and we spent Sunday morning shredding paper and filling big black bags with junk. If Alyssa and Taylor were playing Russia together, I absolutely did not care.

It was happening!

A new room!

But then I looked out the window of my future bedroom and saw Peter and Andrew giving Alyssa and Taylor skateboarding lessons. I stood there, perfectly still, long enough that Mom came to the window to see what I was looking at. I said, "Why didn't somebody come get me?"

Somebody like Peter.

Mom said, "Do you want to go over?"

Right then the whole gang went inside Alyssa's house, and I knew I'd lost my chance to join in. I couldn't exactly go ring her bell.

"No," I managed. "I don't think I do."

"Good. Because I was thinking we're just about ready to hit the mall."

So we went to the mall and mostly I wanted to just crawl into one of the model beds at the store and sleep until it was, I don't know, time to go away to college? Or at least until the day and hour of the Russia showdown had come and gone and Alyssa had either died or moved or stopped caring about this bizarre series of Cold Wars we'd been fighting all summer.

Maybe the cicadas knew *exactly* what they were doing.

How could Peter do that to me? Go hang out at her house when he hadn't even called me about watching the new *End of Daze* together or anything?

And the weekend was practically over!

I pushed aside all Darcy Lane drama and threw myself into our mission.

I found a display with a bedspread set I really liked— just colorful circles upon circles—and when Mom liked it, too, I found the right size on the shelves. We got new sheets and curtains, and Mom got in line to pay for it all.

Right near the register, by one of the fancy living room setups, I saw a framed poster of a single orange flower that I really liked, maybe because it reminded me of that red flower my mother had sat by when she'd told me my life would be full of adventures. So I pointed it out to Mom and she said okay to that, too.

I went and got one out of a small stack leaning against a wall, and brought it over to the checkout. Since there were still three people ahead of us, I ran through the store and found a jewelry box I adored—a plain white wooden cube with a glass top that let you peek inside to its soft lavender compartments. I thought maybe I'd pass the ballerina one on to Isabel the next time I saw her.

"I want you to do something for me," Mom said as we left the store with our heavy bags. "It's an assignment."

"Mom!"

"Just hear me out." She started putting stuff into the trunk, and I had a flash of wondering about who or what was going to be in the trunk of that car on *End of Daze*. It was all I could do not to ask Mom.

She said, "I want you to take a sheet of paper and write down everything you like about Taylor and Alyssa. As friends. One list for each of them."

I groaned. "I *really* don't feel like doing that."

"Then don't make a list, but at least *think* about it. Okay?"

"Fine," I said, and we got into the car.

When we got home the house smelled funny. Mom said, "I think your dad has a surprise for you."

I ran upstairs and into my new room, where Dad stood with a paint roller. The walls were the most gorgeous pale lavender I'd ever seen and something about the paint made the carpet—wall-to-wall cream—look even better.

"I love it!" I spun around to take in all four walls.

"Your mom thought you would," Dad said.

The only bad thing about it was that we had to let the paint dry and air out the room for a few days before I could actually move in. I couldn't stand the wait.

It was already nearly dark by the time we finished dinner, but I wandered over to Taylor's house anyway to ask her to come over and see the lavender. But Taylor's mom answered the door, looking confused.

"She's at Alyssa's?" she said. "The sleepover?"

"Of course!" I actually smacked myself on the head to really make a show of it. "I forgot."

I sat on my front porch for a while taking calming breaths. I watched for shadows at Alyssa's window and saw nothing—no lights, no shadows—but I was looking at the wrong place. They'd be in the back room, with the Ouija board and peep show. I pictured sleeping bags, flashlights.

I wanted to be there almost as badly as I was glad I wasn't.

I was going to beat Alyssa at Russia if it killed me.

18.

In the car on the way to camp on Monday, I couldn't exactly ask Peter about his visit to Alyssa's with his mom right there, so I waited until we got out, and said, "I saw you teaching Alyssa how to skateboard."

"What?" Peter scratched his head. "Oh, right. That." He snorted. *"Barely."*

I couldn't make eye contact and looked at the ground. The bugs were mostly gone from the air, but their deathly remains were still hanging around, gathering in wispy piles along the curb. "So you like her now?"

"Julia," he said, all serious, and he shook his head.

So I just walked away and looked for Laney and pulled her into the girls' bathroom and told her about Taylor and Alyssa having a sleepover without me. "And I asked Peter if he would teach me how to skateboard, and then this weekend he was teaching Alyssa instead."

"But he likes you; I just know it!" Laney rubbed my back. "And anyway, after you beat her at Russia, he'll never even give her another thought."

"It's just a game." I went into a stall to get some toilet paper so I could blow my nose.

"Everything's a game," Laney said. "And you have to play it. So when you ride home with him today, you have to act like you don't care."

I knew she had to be right—she sounded so very sure—and still it didn't feel right to play games with Peter.

We were learning a set of pieces called *The Carnival of the Animals* for the big concert, and the music was so lovely and so sad that I had a hard time holding it together. I didn't dare look across the room to where Peter sat with his trumpet. He couldn't like Alyssa. He wouldn't. But I felt crazy about it. Because boys like Peter *had* to like girls like me—and *not* girls like Alyssa—or there was no hope at all.

When Peter tried to talk to me at lunch, I acted like I was really in a rush and had to practice some hard clarinet parts and we'd just talk later. And when we met at the usual spot in the parking lot at the end of the day to wait for our ride, he said, "About Alyssa . . ."

I said, "Oh that."

My mom was already pulling up.

"Forget I mentioned it," I said. "You can hang out with anybody you want to, right?"

"Julia," he moaned.

"What," I said. "It's true."

"I thought it would be a few more years before this started."

"Before what started?" I breathed hard.

He adjusted his backpack straps on the shoulders of his purple tee. "Before you started to get weird."

"What are you talking about?"

"Everyone says girls get nutty." He made that crazy gesture by the side of his head. "They get boy-crazy and mean and stuff. I didn't think it would happen to you, but if it did, I thought it would at least be a few years from now."

None of this was my fault. Didn't he see?

I said, "Yeah, well, me, too, I guess."

We didn't talk the whole way home.

At home, Mom pulled hamburgers and hot dogs out of the fridge. "Taylor's coming for dinner," she said. "In case you forgot."

I absolutely had forgotten. I wasn't sure I'd even been told. I said, "Does she have to?" and Mom might have smiled.

"Yes, she has to. Her parents have a work party to go to."

"I'm just really tired."

"Yeah, well, join the club."

Then the phone rang and it was Taylor's mom, and she said she'd made other arrangements and not to worry. And that felt worse.

We had burgers and dogs and macaroni salad out at the table on the deck, then moved some of my furniture into the room so we wouldn't have to do it all at once. It still reeked of paint, but after my parents went back downstairs, I sat there, barefoot on the floor, breathing it all in.

19.

Before I knew it, it was Thursday—the last full day of camp since Friday was just the concert. And now that camp was over, I wished it had been longer. How would I survive the rest of the summer—the rest of my *life*—without Laney?

"This *really* stinks," I said, when she was watching me practice elevensies by the parking lot.

"We need cell phones," Laney said. "So we can at least stay in touch, like, constantly."

"I'll work on it." I nodded.

"Me, too," she said. "And stop looking at your hands. You know how to *clap* without looking!"

I threw another ball, but I wasn't trying very hard. Great as Laney was, I missed having Peter as my coach. We weren't exactly ignoring each other anymore, but he wasn't going out of his way to be around a nutty girl like me. Right now he was waiting for our ride as far away from me as was possible while still being able to see me.

"Do you think if you win, you'll win Taylor back?" Laney asked. I'd told her it was all on again, for Saturday.

But it wasn't even about that anymore.

Was it ever?

"I don't know." I thought hard about what I wanted to be different after the showdown. "If I could have anything I wanted, I wish I never had to see either of them ever again. Then I'd like to never meet another girl like Alyssa in my whole life."

"They're everywhere." Laney was bouncing a ball. She had no real interest in Russia beyond helping me get better. "You need to learn to spot them and stay away. And, I mean, you have friends in school, right?"

"Not great ones," I said. "Taylor actually told me the other day that there was no way I would ever win. Why would she even say that?"

Laney shook her head. "You just have to win and you'll have that to hold over them forever."

I loved this girl.

Loved.

And even though we'd still see each other tomorrow we knew it wouldn't be the same so we hugged hard when my mom pulled into the lot.

In the car, I handed Mom the envelope I'd been given by the camp director after turning in our order form and check that morning: three tickets to the concert.

"You have to call Wendy to remind her," Mom said as she slipped it into her purse.

I very much didn't want to.

I looked out the window to where Laney was pretending to walk down an imaginary flight of stairs behind a small car. I laughed and waved.

"Who's that?" Mom asked, as Peter jogged over and climbed into the backseat.

"That's Laney," I said. "Another clarinet."

"She nice?" Mom asked, after saying hi to Peter.

Now Laney was climbing back up those stairs. "She's entirely awesome."

"Well, that's exciting!" Mom's voice was full of hope.

"She lives on the complete opposite side of the island," I said.

"That's too bad."

"But if I had a cell phone, I'd at least be able to text her and stay in touch!"

Mom hit the gas and we were off. "Peter, do you have a cell phone?" she asked.

"Yes, ma'am," he said, and presented it as evidence. "Just got one."

"See!" I was giddy.

She said, "One battle at a time, Julia," and we all settled in for a quiet drive.

After saying good-bye to Peter in the driveway, I went up to the porch and saw a note taped to the door. I snatched it, unfolded it, and read it: *Saturday. 1:00 p.m. No excuses. Even if it's Armageddon.*

"Pretty big word for a girl like Alyssa." Mom was reading over my shoulder.

I turned and looked at her, shocked.

"Sorry," Mom said. "That was mean."

We started cracking up and couldn't stop.

The paint smell was officially gone, so we moved the rest of my stuff in and started to wash my new sheets and bedspread. Too excited to do anything else, I sat in front of the washing machine, watching circles and bubbles go round and round, and thought through a whole game of Russia in my head.

When everything was dry, Mom and I put them all in place, and the whole room felt new and amazing. We hung the orange flower over the bed and both took a step back. I said, "I love it. But the dolls . . ." We'd moved them from my old room to a shelf in the new one. "They have to go."

"But you *love* those dolls," Mom said.

"*Loved*, Mom. When I was like five."

"We'll box them up," she said as she plopped down and had a look around. She seemed sad.

"Mom?" I said.

She looked up.

"Wendy said her mom thought you were going to have another baby, that this was going to be a baby's room." We were in it now, no turning back.

"Oh, honey." She grabbed my hand. "You've been wondering all this time? Why didn't you ask?"

"I'm asking now."

She took a minute to think. "Your father and I had what people call a . . ." She stopped then started again. "We thought I was pregnant, but it was just for a week, and I actually wasn't. But when it was happening, I started getting excited about the idea—everything was so much simpler when you were a baby, and I guess I was thinking a lot about that— so we talked about maybe trying, but we're way too old. And we're fine about it. We're good."

"I think I would have liked a little brother or sister." I felt so sad, imagining a little baby to hold.

"I know it's hard sometimes. You feel like you're on your own. But your father and I, we love things just as they are. And the friend thing. It really does get easier, I swear."

We joked about the idea of Dad changing diapers again, and then she left me alone on my circle-y bed in my cool new room. I felt like big things could happen here. I tried to think ahead, another seventeen years, to imagine what things would be like when the cicadas came back. I'd be twenty-nine, so I'd probably only ever come back to sleep in this room when I was visiting my parents from wherever I lived.

It seemed crazy that it would ever happen.

The phone rang and I stiffened, and Mom called out that it was Taylor. I didn't even want to move to go talk to her, but I did anyway.

"I have something to tell you," she said.

"What?"

"Alyssa and Peter are going to the movies together tonight. I thought you should know."

"Thanks." My face started to vibrate, like it might jump off my skull.

"That was all. I have to go." She hung up.

I went to the mirror and looked at myself, but nothing appeared different even though it was.

I hated Alyssa and it felt good.

I hated Peter and it felt awful.

Mom seemed extra happy that night. She smiled wide and more easily, and she talked about all these things we should do come fall and winter, like apple-picking and ice-skating. She was already giddy about Christmas, and it was only August. I sat close to her while she talked about new decorations that we might get—like a new star topper for our tree—hoping some of it would rub off on me like glitter.

Then the phone rang and Mom picked it up and there was no one there. She hung up and said, "Wrong number," but I could tell in her tone she wasn't convinced, and neither was I.

It rang and rang again and Mom answered once more, but there was no one there.

"Not this again," Dad said, coming into the room.

The next time Mom just picked up the phone and hung it right back up without a word. "I'm going over there," she said.

"Mom! No!" I said.

She looked expectantly at Dad.

"I have to side with Julia on this one." He rubbed his eyes and sighed like he couldn't believe his misfortune at being stuck in the middle of all this. "You've met the girl's mother. You really think she's going to be open to having this conversation after the way she reacted to, well, you know?"

Mom's frustration at knowing he was right, I guess, came out as a deep, guttural scream. What had they even talked about that night?

The phone rang again. I picked it up and just held it to my ear, picturing Alyssa at the movie theater, maybe calling from the bathroom.

"Hello?" came a confused girl's voice. A familiar one.

My brain worked hard to figure it out. "Wendy?"

"Julia?" she said. "I called a second ago, but somebody hung up on me."

"Sorry," I said. "We've been getting some prank calls."

I went out to the deck for some privacy as my parents started talking in the den. Call waiting signed another call, but I ignored it and asked Wendy about her vacation. She told stories about crab cakes and beaches and a big house on the ocean. "Sounds awesome," I said.

"How was camp?" she asked.

"It's been great." And I froze, thinking about the extra ticket. "I mean, it's been okay."

"So what's the deal with the concert tomorrow?"

"Oh." I squeezed my eyes shut. "Let me ask my mom. I'll be right back."

I put the phone down on the table and didn't move a muscle while I tried to think how to play this. The idea of Wendy coming to the concert and of having to introduce her to Laney made me mad. Why had Mom—who I could hear saying to Dad, "well, somebody has to do something about it"—invited her without even asking me? I pictured Wendy talking to Peter, who'd betrayed me, and thought I'd be sick from jealousy. So I made some footstep sounds with my feet and made some muffling noises into my hand, and picked up the phone again. "You there?"

"Yeah."

"My mom's *so sorry* but she totally forgot to get you a ticket. And they're not selling them at the door."

"Oh."

The silence was so painful that I wished for some cicadas to fill it, but they were officially gone. I heard a lone cricket croak, then said, "I'm really sorry."

"No big deal," she said. "We'll make plans soon, though, right?"

"Yeah, definitely." I'd gotten away with it. "Okay, I have to go."

"Okay, bye."

I hit a button on the phone to end the call, and got up and turned to head inside. Mom was standing at the door. I had no idea for how long until I looked her in the eyes.

"I'm not impressed." She turned off the outdoor lights.

"You invited her without asking me," I said, lamely, in the dark.

"Don't even try to make this about me," she said wearily and drifted back into the den.

I got an old notebook out before going to bed and turned to a new page. I wrote down the names *Alyssa* and

Taylor. But when I went to write things under them that
I liked, I found myself writing words like *mean* and *disloyal*
and *stuck up* instead.

On the next page, I wrote *Laney*, and wrote under it,
Awesome in every way.

I wrote down *Peter* and had to think hard.

I wrote *smart*, then *funny, cute, understanding*.

I crossed those all out and wrote, *TRAITOR*.

Under Wendy, I wrote *smart, talented, happy, confident,
nice, nice to me*.

Then I wrote *Julia* and the letters looked funny to me,
like that couldn't possibly be a real word, a real name.

I wondered what words my friends might write under *me*.

20.

We'd been told to wear white shirts and black pants or skirts for the concert, which seemed silly in summer, but those were the rules. So I pulled out my lightest weight black skirt and a short-sleeved white top and got dressed. I spent some extra time on my hair, drying it with the blower, which I hadn't really done all summer, and making it curl under just right.

"You look gorgeous!" Laney said when she saw me, but I didn't feel gorgeous. I felt awful about everything.

Laney was wearing a black skort—!—and a white top with black suspenders. "And *you* can somehow pull off suspenders!" I said. "How is that even possible?"

"Just lucky, I guess." She really had no idea how amazing she was. I didn't dare kill her mood with my drama.

The stage was all set up with the chairs arranged just so, and I stood there in the wings for a minute trying hard not to feel so lousy. I peeked out into the auditorium, which was filling up quickly, and that started to do the trick. Then a few notes played by people tuning their instruments rose up, making me excited and nervous at the same time. Which was silly. There was nothing to be nervous about. Even if I messed up, who'd even know but me? Still, it felt important.

To do a good job.

Since I'd gone and mucked things up good last night.

There is a moment, after the curtain opens, right after the conductor raises his hands or his pick, when the whole band, the whole world, seems to be holding its breath. But it is not *holding*, it is *waiting to inhale*.

Someone might cough in the audience, someone might whisper to the person next to them, but the band doesn't hear any of that, not in any real way. The band is waiting, poised, so that it can take that one last inhale before every-thing takes off and the rest of the concert is like a runaway train, no brakes.

I savored that moment, that pause before the inhale, thinking that it was possible it would be the moment before everything really changed, before *I* changed somehow and for good.

It was definitely our best performance of *The Carnival of the Animals*, and when this one part came during the piece called *Aquarium*, right after a clarinet solo that Laney played brilliantly, and the horns swelled, I seriously thought I was going to cry. Because I'd nailed it and I guess a lot of other people had, too, because it felt like we all had.

During the applause I looked out at the audience and saw my parents, with that empty seat next to them, and I thought about Wendy and felt bad about making fun of her, even if only in my head, for stickers and wanting to play duets. At least she was passionate about stuff. Like I was, like Laney was. Peter, too.

Alyssa and Taylor didn't seem passionate about anything.

Not even Russia, not really.

When we all got up to take a bow at the end of the show, I felt like I had on the skyscraper that day—so small that I was large at the same time. I had to work really hard to get control of the muscles in my face, and I didn't dare look across the way at Peter and his trumpet because I knew that would make me lose it.

Laney reached over and squeezed my hand, and I squeezed hers back.

When I saw my parents in the lobby, I ran to Mom and she hugged me. I couldn't fight tears any longer.

"I'm so sorry," I said. "About Wendy."

She hugged me harder and said, "I know you are, Julia. I know you are."

"And I'm so glad you signed me up for camp, and I'm sorry I was such a jerk about it."

She pulled back and said, "You know your father and I are just doing our best."

I nodded, wiping away tears.

We saw Laney in the parking lot and introduced our parents. Both our dads had taken the afternoon off, and our moms were instantly chatty. Then Laney and I hugged good-bye. "You'll keep in touch, right?" I asked.

"Of course, you dope." She hugged me again. "We can email! Or even send letters! It'll be hip and old-fashioned. And they have to get us phones *eventually*. I mean, what is this, the Dark Ages?"

Pulling out of our hug, she flashed that smile of hers that made you want to *be* her. "And *promise me* you'll remember that when you get to elevens you have to keep your eye on the ball and just trust that you can clap all fancy *without actually looking at your hands*, right?"

I laughed. "I'll remember."

We went out to lunch as a celebration, down at a nice restaurant on the bay. Right after we sat down, Peter and his family walked in. He smiled at me, and he looked so cute with his tie still on that I thought maybe things weren't so bad. Even if it was true about him going to a movie with Alyssa, I felt too bighearted and full to hold it against him right this second. Nobody suggested combining tables, and I was a little bit sad, but it wasn't up to me.

When we were done with our entrées, Peter came over, said hello, and slid into the empty seat next to me. "Big day tomorrow, huh?"

"Yeah," I said. "I guess Alyssa told you when you were at the movies."

"Um." He tilted his head. "Huh?"

"Taylor said that you and Alyssa went to a movie last night."

Peter made a face. "Not that I'm aware of."

"Oh," I said.

"She asked me, and I said no."

I couldn't help it; I smiled and let my gaze drift toward my parents. They were talking happily, laughing at the silly names of boats docked just outside the restaurant.

Leaning in to Peter, I said, "I'm *dying* to know what's in that trunk." I pinched his arm. "You made me wait all weekend."

"We'll watch soon." His face brightened. "Hey, you want cake?"

I must have looked confused because he said, "My birthday."

"Oh, happy birthday! Sure."

"What about your parents?"

"Mom," I said. "Do you guys want cake? It's Peter's birthday."

"No, you go. Happy birthday, Peter!"

So I went and sat at Peter's table with his parents. We split a piece, he and I, because we were both too full already. Then it was time for checks to be paid and for us to go to separate cars and houses.

"You'll be there tomorrow?" I asked as we walked through the parking lot.

"Wouldn't miss it," he said, and he gave me a high five, grabbing my hand as we hit and holding it for a long second.

Taylor was sitting on her front porch reading when I got home, and I asked Mom if I could go over for a minute.

"You sure?"

I nodded and wondered when Taylor's sister was

coming home, whether she'd missed Taylor at all. "She seems lonely."

It was the truth and it seemed to hit some soft spot in my mom because she nodded.

So I went over even though I knew Taylor was probably going to think I looked like a geek in my band clothes.

"You're reading?" I took a seat next to her.

"Yes, Julia. I read."

I just nodded.

"Alyssa was looking for you." Taylor turned down the corner of a page and put the book down behind her. "She wants to make sure you got her note."

"Yeah. I got it."

"I'm tired of this whole Russia thing." Taylor stretched her legs out in front of her. "What is it with you two anyway?"

I almost laughed but just shook my head. Because, really: What *was* it? Could I ever explain it? Did I even understand it? The way you just feel in your bones when you and another human being are just never going to be able to connect, no matter how hard you try. It was a mystery I wasn't sure I'd ever crack.

"We had a fight," Taylor said. "Me and Alyssa."

"About *what*?" I tried not to get too excited.

"She dared me to go skinny-dipping when Peter and Andrew were there, and I said no, and she called me a prude."

"Oh," I got stuck on the idea of Peter skinny-dipping at

Alyssa's house. "Did *they* all do it?"

"Andrew got in and took his shorts off but for like two seconds, and you couldn't see anything, not that I was looking." Taylor looked at me superseriously, as if to make sure that last bit sunk it. "And Peter just said no way, no how." She shook her head. "But she didn't call *him* a prude." She sighed. "Anyway, she just wouldn't stop talking about it, so I told her to shut up, and she told me to eff off, only she didn't say eff." She pulled her legs back up close to her body. "That's it."

"Crazy." I tried not to smile. "But for the record, I wouldn't have done it either."

"Well, I *know that*, Julia."

"She's been prank calling my house. Just calling and hanging up."

Taylor didn't move an inch, and only said, "I honestly don't think she cares enough about you to do something like that."

"I can't explain it," I said.

Taylor got up to go inside.

When my parents went into the living room for *End of Daze*, I said good night. And even though I was happy to be spending the evening settling into my new room, I was pretty grateful that *End of Daze* was only a miniseries, not an ongoing thing, and that my parents wouldn't have this secret thing between them once summer was done. If it meant that Peter and I wouldn't have our secret for long either, that was okay. At the rate we were watching, I wasn't even sure we'd make it to the end.

I climbed into bed with my book, and I read and read and reached the scene where the truth about the face in the haunted pond—who it was, why it was there, everything— was about to be revealed. But the strangest thing happened. Right as I got to the very line where I was sure the old man who lived in the woods was going to blow the whole thing wide open, right as the girl and the cripple were going to have their life together changed forever, I closed the book.

I got up and put it on my bookshelf.

I didn't want to know if the whole thing was somehow a trick of the eye or, worse, a hoax.

Life was long and there was plenty of time to stop believing stuff later.

I sort of missed that unicorn poster.

When I still couldn't sleep a few hours later, after my parents had come up and gone to bed, I got up and put on a sweatshirt over my pajamas. I went downstairs, turned on one of the lights in the backyard, and went outside to practice Russia. I was up to twelvesies when a light came on in Peter's room. A minute later, his window opened and his head popped out. "Are you crazy?" he whisper-yelled.

"I think I am!" I said back, not even trying to whisper.

"*Shhhhh.* I'm coming over."

A few minutes later, I heard the back door of his house creak open. Soon he was at the fence, climbing and dropping down into my yard. "Julia," he said. "It's late. You're going to wake up the whole neighborhood."

"So?" I threw the ball way high and did the over-and-under leg clap and caught it. Only three more times to go before I hit the final move of the game.

But then noises came from my own house, and Mom appeared on the deck in her bathrobe. "Peter. I don't want to have to wake your mom."

"Sorry." He climbed back up over the fence and was gone.

I was about to tell Mom that I needed a few more minutes, and that it wasn't up to her to tell me to stop, but she stood there and folded her arms. "So, how hard is it?"

I did another eleven. "Not that hard."

"Are you any good at it?"

"Pretty good." I bounced the ball and caught it, not as a move, just for something to do.

"Good enough to win?"

"I don't know."

She turned a lawn chair to face the patio where I was practicing and turned another of the backyard lights on, "Show me what you've got."

I started from the beginning again and breezed through the early steps. When they started getting harder, Mom started saying things like, "Try that one again. Another seven times." And, "That one you've got, no problem. Just keep your eye on the ball and not on your hands."

"Mom?" I said, smiling and thinking of Laney. "What's going on?"

"What do you mean?"

I bounced my ball and caught it. "Why the sudden interest in Russia?"

"Oh, no reason."

Dad came out, too, and pulled up a chair next to Mom but abandoned it in favor of grabbing an extra ball and trying to learn the game alongside me. He dropped it about a gazillion times before Mom said, "You're hopeless."

"Just rusty," Dad said.

I was doing tensies so he tried it. "This is harder than it looks."

"Julia makes it look easy," Mom said.

"You want to try?" He held a ball out to her.

"No, thanks." She giggled. "I'm fine here."

"But you used to play Leansies Clapsies!" I said.

"A lifetime ago," she said.

They coached me all the way through to the end three times before we called it quits.

"You can do this, Julia," Mom said solemnly when we went inside.

I nodded that I knew, but I also felt a little bit scared. When I was the only one who cared, the Russia showdown was already a big enough deal. If Mom was counting on me—if she thought that now we had something to prove together—I thought maybe I was doomed.

21.

It was so hot Saturday, and so humid, that I thought I might just rather die than go through with any of this. The morning crawled toward lunchtime, and I didn't really feel much like eating, so I faked it for Mom's sake and did some stretches, which seemed ridiculous even to me since I'd never done them before.

When it was nearly one, I waited on the front porch until Alyssa came out of her house with a ball in her hand. Before getting up to walk across the street, I took a few deep, calming breaths, and it was like the whole summer flashed before my eyes. The first glimpse of the pink chair. The skyscraper view and skyscraper girl. The Ouija board saying "yes." Peter. The woods. The cicada infestation. I couldn't remember what the bugs had sounded like or what it felt like not to wear a bra all day.

Alyssa was wearing the same outfit she'd had on the first day I met her, and for some reason that felt right.

"So you showed," she said when I met her by her garage.

"Of course I showed."

"And here comes our ref." I turned and saw Andrew walking across the street. Behind him, Peter was on his skateboard. A few of the other neighborhood kids came out of the woodworks, and I wondered if any of them had any idea what was at stake here, whether they'd heard stories about the prank calls, whether Alyssa had been bragging all over town.

Alyssa's mother came out and sat on their front porch. Even some of the local dragonflies seemed to want in on the action, flying lazily around in the thick air. I hated dragonflies and their quick darting movements, and I worked to block them out the same way I was trying to block out all the spectators. I'd told my parents that they were only allowed to watch from our porch—out of my line of sight across the street.

"You ready?" Alyssa asked, just as Taylor wandered over from her house and sat on the curb by Alyssa's.

"Ready." I felt it.

"All right." Andrew adjusted his baseball cap. "You both know the rules."

"Just make sure she doesn't cheat," Alyssa said.

"Make sure *she* doesn't," I said.

"I know, I know." Andrew already seemed bored. "So I guess, on your mark—"

I rubbed my thumb over the ball in my hand as Alyssa and I both turned to face the garage.

"Get set."

Peter said, "Good luck, Julia," and I felt like I was the only one who heard it.

"Go!"

Alyssa and I both threw against the garage and caught, then did twosies with the bounce inside the line, and caught. After that, we both moved away from the garage and into the street for threesies, and I started to get distracted by things people were saying. Like, "How many moves are there?" and "What's the prize?" To block them out I started playing *Aquarium* in my head and went on to foursies.

The first time I made it through the song, I was finishing up fivesies. Somehow the rhythm of the music in my head and the counting of notes and bars all worked to help the count of Russia. I stopped to see Alyssa already on sixies, and I started the song in my head again and started sixies, too. I'd been thinking that dropping the ball was my worst enemy, but if Alyssa finished faster, I'd still lose, even with a perfect game.

"Stop humming," Alyssa said a few seconds later.

THE BATTLE OF DARCY LANE

I hadn't even realized I'd been doing it. I stopped to wipe some sweat off my rib cage under my shirt, and Peter came over and handed me a bottle of water. I took a swig, smiled, and handed it back.

"You've got this," he said.

I've got this, I repeated in my head and got back into the zone and stayed there—bouncing, clapping, throwing, turning, whacking, catching. Like I'd been born knowing how to do it.

It seemed like it took no time at all before Alyssa and I were already at twelvesies. That's when things started to move as if in slow motion. We fell into this rhythm where we were taking turns, and when we were up to nine each, going on ten, Alyssa said, "Taylor slept over last night. That's like the second time in two weeks."

My ball was in the air, and I felt my balance shift but caught it anyway—ten down, two to go.

She seemed to just be standing there, waiting for me to reply, so I took the chance to throw my eleventh out of twelve. And while the ball was in the air, I thought about people like Laney, how probably there were a lot of them out there, people I'd meet in life and *like*.

I caught it.

And with Alyssa still waiting, I thought about saying maybe the nastiest thing that I could think of, even if it was just flat-out calling her the same thing she'd called me in the woods that day. But Peter called out, "You're doing great, Julia. Stay focused."

Right then Alyssa threw her last of twelve—too high. She spun and looked up, squinting into the sun, holding out her hands—too late.

She missed.

The ball bounced to the curb.

Some people moaned. Some people cheered. Taylor turned her head away. But above it all, I heard Alyssa's mother's voice, and I could see her face turn sour-looking when she said, "Losing to a loser makes you a loser, Lyss. Come ON!"

My parents appeared on our porch, and I wanted to wave but didn't want to confuse my muscles by doing anything out of the ordinary, anything non-Russia. I was so grateful they weren't the kind of parents who would drop me off at the house of a neighbor they didn't even know. So grateful that they *were* the kind of parents who at least *told me* not to judge people based on their freckles or hair or weight or coolness, even if I was still coming up short.

"You can do this," Mom had said, and the words were echoing inside me when I threw the ball high and did the under-the-leg clapping thing for the twelfth time.

I caught it.

I took a deep breath as a few people clapped and Peter held out the water again. I went to him and took a long draw off it. I felt like I was maybe dying.

"You okay?" Peter asked.

"Yeah. Good."

"I know you can do this." He squeezed my shoulder gently.

"Me, too." I nodded.

"But I'll still hang out with you if you don't," he said.

"Gee, thanks."

My first few spins for thirteen made me a little dizzy, and I had to blink a few times to catch my balance.

"Pace yourself," Peter called out. "I'll let you know if she's really on your tail."

I did my third and fourth turn and felt good.

My parents came down onto the street when I was on my seventh spinning move, and I realized I actually wanted them there, closer. They clapped and Mom said, "You're doing great, Julia."

Alyssa's mom said, "Dammit, Alyssa. Hurry up!"

Mom called out, "There's really no need for that kind of language, is there?"

If there was any reply, I didn't hear it.

I was up to my ninth throw when Peter said, "No reason to rush, Julia. But she's up to nines, okay, so just keep going slow and steady."

"Who's this guy?" Alyssa's mother asked. "Alyssa, HURRY!"

"Julia," Mom said. "Laney called to wish you good luck."

"Mom," I said. "Give me some room, okay?"

She said, "Sorry," and backed off a bit.

"Who's *Laney*?" It was the first time Alyssa had spoken in at least several minutes. "Your girlfriend?"

I stopped, frozen still, and stared at her.

Exhibit A.

I pictured her small and trapped under a glass and wondered if that was what her life felt like for real.

She stared back.

"Where do you even get this stuff?" I asked.

"What?" Alyssa also stopped her game.

She looked so nasty to me that I couldn't even remember why I'd ever even tried to be her friend, why I'd ever let her make me feel bad or scared. I said, "You just say the most ridiculous stuff sometimes."

She made her lips pouty and looked around. Then she just made a puffing sound and said, "Whatever, Julie."

So I puffed, too. "Whatever, Alicia."

"Alyssa!" her mom called out.

"Mom! Just *shut up*!" Alyssa yelled back and everything got incredibly quiet.

I had one more thirteen to do for the win. With Peter there and Laney out there somewhere and the lingering orchestra swell in my head, I knew that my last throw was going to be the easiest thing in the world.

Like even a monkey could do it.

So I went for it.

I threw the ball, and I spun around, and I clapped in front—

and I could feel the sweat of my left hand meeting the
sweat of my right—and I clapped in back—and kept my eye
on the ball because only an idiot can't clap without looking—
and clapped in front and held my hands out, almost like in
prayer—and I felt the hard smack of the ball on my palms.

My parents cheered.

Alyssa's mother said, "Unbelievable," and went inside.

Alyssa just stood there, looking mad, and said, "You said
it yourself. It's a dumb game." She dropped her ball, and
it rolled to the curb as she walked away.

Taylor stood up and said, "Well, you did it," and strolled
back to her house.

I'd really done it.

Peter rushed over, pulled me into a hug, and
screamed, "YES!"

22.

He came back to my house, and we went straight through the front door and out the back and jumped into the pool with our clothes on.

Instant, cold relief.

Peter said, "That. Was. Awesome."

"I can't believe it." I popped an inflatable tube over my head and began bobbing with my arms crossed in front of me. My shorts were floating up around my thighs.

"Well, I can." Peter dunked his head under.

Then we just floated around for a while, reliving some of the best parts of the morning, and also the weird parts.

"Her mom's pretty intense," Peter said at one point.

"Yeah." I felt bad for Alyssa, but only so much.

"What the heck happened to your garden?" Peter asked, after a while.

I looked over. In a matter of weeks, my poor garden had fallen into chaos. Splitting overripe tomatoes dangled too close to the ground on vines that needed staking. Weeds towered over my pepper plants. "I guess I forgot about it."

Peter hopped off his raft, and his wet purple T-shirt clung to him. He pulled it away with a sucking sound. "Come on. I'll help."

We started pulling weeds and picking the ripe stuff, and I got to thinking about a younger Peter digging in the woods. "Hey, so how did you find out that the treasure wasn't real? That your brother had put it there?"

Peter wiped his forehead, and his hand left a smudge of dirt there. "He told me, the idiot. He couldn't even last an hour without telling me it was just a big joke."

"But why would he *do* that?" I shook my head. "It's so mean."

"I don't know." He was patting some soil near the base of tomato plant. "But I think he felt *really bad* afterward, by how upset I was."

"Maybe he was jealous." I'd just pulled a red pepper off a plant and the air smelled sweet.

"Of *what*?"

I rubbed some dirt off the pepper. "That something exciting was happening to you."

"But it was fake." Peter wiped dirt from his hands, brushing them together.

"But you *thought* it was real."

Peter stood up and stretched. "I'm not sure you're making sense."

I stood, too, lifting the basket of veggies. "Me neither." But I knew I was onto something.

"I'll tell you one thing I know for sure, Julia." Peter stretched his back.

"Yeah?" Was this flirting? "What's that?"

"When I do get around to going to a movie with a girl"—he hooked an arm around my shoulders as we went inside—"I most definitely want it to be you."

Peter planted a kiss on my cheek.

I called Laney after Peter went home and squealed, "He kissed me on the cheek!"

"But did you *win*?" she asked.

"Yes!"

"Of course you did!" Her voice sounded close. "Tell me everything!"

So I told her about the game and the kiss—every last detail—and then we talked for almost an hour about silly things like what kinds of dogs we liked and why we hated our hair.

My parents ordered Chinese food for dinner as a treat, and we ate outside while fireflies, probably glad—like me—to have seen the last of the cicadas for seventeen years, blinked in the yard. I was so happy that it almost made me sad, because summer was ending and school was starting and there'd be homework and Halloween and then winter and snow.

"For the record," Mom said, with an eggroll in her hand, "we'd be just as proud of you if you hadn't won, Julia. It's just a game."

I had some lo mein in my mouth and decided to chew and swallow before I said, "But it's better that I won."

We all smiled, especially Mom, who laughed and said, "It really is."

Later, after dinner, I took a long bath and lay on my bed in my pajamas, feeling tired but also happy. Spying Snow White up on a high shelf, I grabbed Dopey and went downstairs. Mom was in the kitchen, writing something on a notepad.

I put the pieces on the table and sat down.

"Yikes," Mom said, ripping her note off the pad. "What happened to Dopey?"

"An unfortunate accident," I said. "We have any Krazy Glue?"

"Check the junk drawer," she replied. I got up and opened the drawer near the fridge and found a small tube.

"I'll be right back," Mom said, and she left the house walking at a quick pace, sliding her note into an envelope as she went.

I went to the notepad and found a pencil in the junk drawer. Turning the tip on its wide side, I lightly ran it back and forth across the blank page so that the impression her writing had left appeared as white letters. When I'd covered the whole thing, I set the pencil down and read:

> Be mindful of your bedroom
> window and state of undress.
> People (children!) can see in.
>
> Signed,
> A Friendly Neighbor

I tore the paper off the pad, put it in the trash, and went back to the table, not knowing where to even begin with Dopey. I thought about asking Dad for help, but he was in the den with a baseball game on and, also, it seemed like something I should be able to figure out.

A minute later, the front door opened and Mom sat down at the table with me.

She held up two pieces of Dopey's purple hat.

I lined the edges with glue.

23.

On Sunday, I mostly hung out in my room, getting
everything organized, throwing away old clothes and
other things I'd outgrown. Taylor came over when I was
walking a bag of trash out to the curb.

"What's new?" she asked me as she followed me up to
the porch. We sat on the swing.

"Nothing much."

What was *new*? I'd beaten Alyssa was what was new.

When she didn't immediately say anything else, I said,
"Is she mad?"

"Yeah." Taylor sounded bored. "But she's gone."

"What do you mean gone?"

"Jamaica. Some crazy expensive resort. For like two
weeks or something. A big company retreat for her

dad's job. She's so lucky."

This was all great material for a game of Millionaire, but all I could think to say was, "Why would anyone want to go to Jamaica in August?"

Taylor huffed. "Because it's gorgeous, Julia."

This was a ridiculous conversation, and yet I couldn't stop it. "But it must be like a million degrees!"

"You know"—the whites of Taylor's eyes seemed extra bright—"just because somebody isn't *exactly like you* doesn't mean they're not a good person."

"All right. So she's not a bad person." I turned away and rolled my eyes. So maybe nothing had changed.

"I'm not just talking about Alyssa."

"Well, then who?" The girl was making no sense.

"Forget it," Taylor said. Then we both sat there for a while. Finally she said, "What should we do today?"

"Anything but Russia."

"Agreed."

We went inside and asked my mom if she'd take us bowling or to a movie or, well, anything.

That was pretty much how the next two weeks passed: Mom and I getting ready for school, stealing last bits of summer fun—sometimes with Taylor, sometimes without. Like we went to the beach a few times, and waded in the waves and built sand castles. We went to see my grandparents—my dad's—at their lake house a few hours away, and I got to ride a pontoon boat and fish. In between, Peter and I planned to catch up on *End of Daze* before the big finale, but somehow we never got around to it. We were too busy floating milk-carton boats on the pond and plowing through the summer reading list, and, of course, he was giving me skateboarding lessons. When *End of Daze* finally ended, everyone seemed happier for it. In our house, we decided that Friday night was going to become a family dinner-and-a-movie night. (My idea.)

Everything seemed so great during these two blissful, Alyssa-free, postwar weeks that I asked Mom if I could have a little end-of-summer bash the day before school started. I invited Taylor, Peter, Andrew, and Wendy, plus Laney—we'd squeed when her mom said yes.

And everybody got along *really well*. We did dives and cannonballs and ate watermelon and had a tetherball tournament, and when Wendy and Laney ganged up on me during Marco Polo, I didn't mind one bit.

"I seriously don't see what all the fuss was about," Laney said to me in a whisper about midway through. "Taylor's a little bit . . . dull?"

I might have laughed a little too loudly when I checked to see whether Taylor had heard. Then Laney said,

"Wendy, on the other hand, is really cool."

I felt so very foolish about so very many things but also hopeful about the year ahead.

Mom had made ice pops out of fruit juice, and by the time we were all saying good-bye, we were sticky and chlorinated and goose-bumped from too much time in the pool. It felt like how it should on the last day of summer vacation.

That night we had one call that was a hang-up.

Then another.

Then another.

Each ring was like a hammer to my head, a fist to the gut. And I looked across the street and saw lights on at Alyssa's—different ones than the light they'd put on a timer while they were away—and felt that sick feeling come back.

Nothing had changed.

Nothing had changed except that Alyssa had gone away.

And now she was back.

The first time, Mom picked up and said "Hello?" then hung up and walked away. The second time, she picked up the phone, hung it up, and held it. She did that the third time, too.

After that one, she looked at me. "Did something happen today that I somehow missed?"

"No!" I said. "But Alyssa's back."

The next time the ringing started, I grabbed the phone from Mom and answered. "You don't scare me anymore," I said. "Taylor and I are friends again, and there's nothing you can do to change that."

We'd spent two weeks just the two of us.

We'd joked that maybe Alyssa had fallen off a cliff in Jamaica and wasn't coming back.

The line clicked dead.

"Tread carefully here, Julia," Mom said.

"What do you mean?" I waited for the ringing to start again, thinking about what I'd say this time.

Mom just silently unplugged the phone.

Usually on the night before the first day of school, I had a hard time falling asleep. But this time I nodded off easily, thinking happy things.

Everything was going to be fine and Alyssa would see; Mom would, too.

I hadn't only won the battle; I had won the war.

24

Mother Nature had clearly gotten the memo about school being back in session because I woke up to a cool, crisp morning. Instant fall. I showered, got dressed, checked the clock in my room, and knew that Taylor would be ringing the bell in about ten minutes.

I went downstairs and had a Pop-Tart and joked with Mom about how much she was going to miss spending all day with me and how I was not going to help her grade papers this year. After I brushed my teeth, checked my hair in the mirror again, and repacked the stuff in my backpack, I looked at the clock. It was seven minutes past the time when Taylor usually came and got me for the walk to the bus stop.

Mom looked at the clock, too. "Honey, I think you're going to miss the bus."

"But Taylor always comes and gets me."

"Come on." Mom took a swig of coffee and picked up her keys. "I'll drive you to the bus stop. We can just make it."

"But what about Taylor?" I knew I sounded desperate.

"Taylor is her mother's problem," she said flatly.

We hurried to the car and she backed out of the driveway super fast and spilled coffee on the car's center console. She sped up to the bus stop, rolling through two stop signs on the way.

We made it just in time.

Just in time to see Alyssa and Taylor strolling up to the bus doors arm-in-arm. They were wearing the same shade of lip gloss—a red color I'd never seen Taylor wear before—and matching string bracelets that looked in some vague way Jamaican clung to their left wrists.

If I was going to make the bus, I would have to bolt out of the car and run, shouting, "Wait for me!"

I popped my door open and put one leg on the ground, but then I could hear Taylor saying, "And she said, 'Taylor and I are friends again, and there's nothing you can do about it.'"

Alyssa laughed.

The bus doors closed.

And I could . . . not . . . move.

Taylor had made last night's calls. Maybe even all of them.

My head hurt, trying to make sense of it.

Taylor had made the calls.

Taylor who'd said, "Not everybody has to be like you," and "yes, I read, Julia."

Mom put the car in gear again. "I'll drive you."

"But you'll be late." It was Mom's first day back, too.

"We don't really have any other options."

I closed the door and let go of the door handle and exhaled and watched as houses and trees and lampposts whirred by my window. I wondered what Laney was doing right now. Whether she was already having a better first day of school than I was.

"Do you think Laney could come over again sometime?" I asked.

"Of course," Mom said. "We'll find a way."

When I looked over at her because of a weird sound she made, I saw tears coming out from under her sunglasses.

"Mom?"

She shook her head, pressed her lips together, and wiped tears away with one hand. "I could *kill them*." Her voice was deep and shaky. "I could seriously *kill* them."

I should have felt the same way. I knew that. But I didn't.

I'd beat Alyssa at her game, and it hadn't changed anything.

And nothing I could do ever would.

She would never like me, and I would never like her, and I was through being Taylor's yo-yo friend. Maybe I'd hurt her feelings along the way, the same way she'd hurt mine. The way I'd hurt Wendy, even if she didn't know the whole of it.

It didn't matter.

"Life is so long, honey," Mom said. "*So long.* Ten, twenty years from now, you'll barely be able to remember their names."

I looked out the window as tons of kids milled around my school. I remembered the feeling I'd had during the Russia showdown, when I'd gotten to thirteen. The way the movement itself, the spin and the clap altogether, had felt celebratory, joyous. The way Peter had been watching so hard. The way I knew he, and maybe everybody else, was rooting for me.

Maybe I'd find someone like Laney at school this year— someone *like* me, or at least more like me than Taylor ever was and Alyssa ever would be. Grown-ups didn't have best friends that lived next door. They had neighbors. That was what Taylor and Alyssa were and that was it.

I was pretty sure I would always remember their names no matter what Mom said, but it suddenly seemed possible that in a year or two or ten I'd forget how to play Russia, have no idea whether you had to clap first or turn first or which leg you did what with however many times.

When I got out of the car and closed the door behind me, I waved to Mom and she smiled. "Oh, I almost forgot!"

She handed me her cell phone. "I was ready for a new one, and we're getting rid of the landline. It's a waste of money, really."

I leaned back in through the door to take the phone. "Thanks, Mom."

I knew we'd never talk about why she was really getting rid of the landline, why she was really giving me her phone. I wondered if I'd ever know what she and Alyssa's mom had talked about that night or why my mom had gotten so into the whole Russia showdown, or why she felt the need to write that note to the naked neighbors. Then I wondered whether one day Wendy and I would end up like Mom and Aunt Colleen. Whether we'd look back on all of this and laugh.

"Hey, Julia." Peter's happy face appeared in front of me, and I wondered why everything seemed different for boys, and which of us was luckier. "Who do you have for homeroom?"

I felt twitchy in my fingers and my heart.

I felt like I was already, maybe, forgetting.

Author's Note

How to Play Russia

There is not a lot of evidence out there (on the Internet) that Russia existed as a game, and yet I can assure you that I played it for countless hours during my youth.

Below are the moves of the game, step by step, based on one lone reference I found on the Web and also on my own memory. I recall playing with a tennis ball, but a small rubber ball will also work.

If, at any point during play, you drop the ball or miss a clap or a bounce, you must start again at the beginning. The goal is to complete all the moves without making a single mistake.

Good luck!

1. Throw the ball at a wall and catch it before it hits the ground. ONE TIME.

2. Throw the ball at a wall, let it bounce once between the wall and a line drawn a few feet away, and catch it. TWO TIMES.

3. Throw the ball in the air, clap three times, and catch the ball before it bounces. THREE TIMES.

4.

Throw the ball, twirl your hands around each other four times, then catch the ball before it bounces. FOUR TIMES.

5.

Throw the ball under one leg and catch it before it bounces. FIVE TIMES.

6.

Throw the ball behind your back and up over one shoulder and catch it before it bounces. SIX TIMES.

7.

Throw the ball, turn, clap twice, turn again, and catch the ball after it bounces. SEVEN TIMES.

8.

Throw the ball, bring up your right foot and touch your ankle, bring up your left foot and touch your ankle, and catch the ball after it bounces. EIGHT TIMES.

9.

Throw the ball, spin around, and catch the ball before it hits the ground. NINE TIMES.

10.

Dribble the ball seven times on the ground, slap it off a wall with one hand, and catch it before it bounces. TEN TIMES.

11.

Throw the ball, clap your hands in front of you, then behind your back, then in front of you again, and catch the ball before it bounces. ELEVEN TIMES.

12.

Throw the ball, clap your hands in front of you then under one leg, then once more in front, and catch the ball before it bounces. TWELVE TIMES.

13.

Throw the ball, spin around, then clap front, back and front, then catch before the ball bounces. THIRTEEN TIMES.

acknowledgments

Thanks to:

My editor, Lisa Cheng, for taking a chance on a "quiet" book in an industry that increasingly likes them "loud." Teresa Bonaddio, for the awesome cover. And the rest of the Running Press Kids team.

Emily Jenkins, for an early and enthusiastic read.

My agent, David Dunton, and his daughter Hannah, for cheering Julia's story on.

Jennifer (still Millett to me!) Wilbur and her daughter, Claire, for answering random questions about life as (and with) a twelve-year-old.

Bob, of course.

Nick, always.

And an extra special thanks to the two girls who made my life on Albourne Avenue so miserable. Victory is mine.

aBOUT THE auTHOr

Tara Altebrando is the author of several novels for teens, including *The Best Night of Your (Pathetic) Life* and *Dreamland Social Club*. She is also the co-author of the young adult novel *Roomies* with Sara Zarr. She has, in her lifetime, experienced cicada swarms, mean girls, and countless games of Russia. A graduate of Harvard University, she lives with her husband and two daughters in Queens, New York. For more, visit www.taraaltebrando.com and follow her on Twitter @TaraAltebrando.